A CRYSTAL BALL,
A FABULOUS HEIRLOOM
DIAMOND NECKLACE,
A TAROT CARD
FORETELLING DOOM . . .

What had such exotic things to do with the life of a picture-perfect English village where the most extraordinary event was the vicar's special cream tea?

Far too much! Indeed, once the villagers learned the true identity of their neighbour, they could talk of little else.

What had become of the necklace? What was Mrs. Charles' exact relationship to the strange Cyril Forbes, nicknamed "the Punch and Judy man"? Had the beautiful Edwina Charles really committed a brutal murder? It was up to ex-Detective Chief Superintendent Sayer to silence the flying tongues, to protect the next victim—and to solve two murders instead of one!

Murder Ink.® Mysteries

DEATH IN THE MORNING—Sheila Radley
THE BRANDENBURG HOTEL—Pauline Glen Winslow
McGARR AND THE SIENESE CONSPIRACY—Bartholomew Gill

Scene Of The Crime™ Mysteries

A MEDIUM FOR MURDER—Mignon Warner
DEATH OF A MYSTERY WRITER—Robert Barnard
DEATH AFTER BREAKFAST—Hugh Pentecost

A Scene Of The Crime™ Mystery

A Medium for Murder

Mignon Warner

A DELL BOOK

Published by
Dell Publishing Co., Inc.
1 Dag Hammarskjold Plaza
New York, New York 10017

First published in Great Britain in 1976 as *A Nice Way to Die.*

Dell ® TM 681510, Dell Publishing Co., Inc.

ISBN: 0-440-15245-3

Reprinted by arrangement with David McKay Company, Inc.—Ives Washburn, Inc.

Printed in the United States of America

First Dell printing—October 1980

CHAPTER ONE

The southern approach was the prettiest and had not altered in two centuries—it was still as it had been all that time ago, a picture-postcard English village with a 16th-century church, a pond with ducks and three white swans on it, and in the centre of the old part of the village, a farm with nineteen Friesian cows, all of which had a name and were lovingly tied in their own individual stall in the big barn each night, in the old way.

There were three public houses and a brewery with steam-driven machinery. Fitzsimmons Family Brewery had started out in life as just another farmhouse, but as time progressed and the locals developed a taste and a strong partiality for Farmer Fitzsimmons' home-brew, bits and pieces were hastily and haphazardly tacked on to the original building until today 'The Brewery', as it was known locally, resembled a lopsided house of playing-cards and looked about as fragile, despite the fact that it had stood in its present form, without as much as a loose roofing slate, for almost one hundred and twenty-five years. In the dead of night when there was little moonlight and a strong gusty wind was blowing, it presented quite a chilling spectre and was said, on such a night, to be haunted by the male members of the Fitzsimmons family—four generations of them—who returned to sup the brew which they had made famous in those parts.

Farther on were the neat Council-owned houses and, in a select new development of a dozen or so properties, 'the newcomers'—wealthy retired city folk who had had sprawling bungalows built for themselves and had the time to devote to local affairs and were given to complaining incessantly, and to no avail, about The Mess, the crumbling outbuildings and rusted remains of ancient agricultural machinery which generations of farmers had allowed to accumulate in their fields, wide open to the public gaze.

The population was just under the two thousand mark, and in better times the working men of the village had been employed either on neighbouring farms or in The Brewery. Some were still thus employed, but most—especially the young—were obliged to travel the twenty-five miles to the nearest town, Gidding, where there was a textile factory, to seek employment.

Apart from the church and The Brewery, the only other place of local interest was a freak of nature known as Widow Roth's Stones. Wise men of science had spent years studying their formation and speculating on the true meaning of their existence, and as with fashions, one theory would oust and become more popular than the last. As for the villagers themselves, they listened with a curiously sober detachment to all the theorising and simply went on believing what they had always believed, that the Widow Roth was a high priestess of a local witches' coven and that at the moment of her seizure by the village elders—it was said that she was burnt at the stake—she was laying out the stones either in the performance of or preparatory to performing some ancient diabolic fertility rite. There was, however, no official record of any such person or family with the surname Roth having ever lived in or anywhere near the village: nor was there any written proof or evidence that witchcraft had ever been practised thereabouts.

The pace of life in the village was leisurely and ordered and only once in recent years had anything exciting happened to disturb its tranquility. Its only tangible claim to any sort of fame belonged not so much to the village itself but to three of its one-time inhabitants. The first was James Fitzsimmons, now deceased, the founder of The Brewery; the next, Edward Player, also deceased, a diversified and controversial artist of some considerable note and a recluse who retired to the village in nineteen thirty-eight and whose works were considered by collectors to be most desirable, in particular his grotesque paintings of children. (Edward Player was said to have abominated and despised children and without exception: his only child, it was rumoured, was a mature thirty before he expressed a desire to see her, and then—or so the rumour went—only because he was in failing health and urgently required the selfless care and devoted attention one could not demand or expect from someone other than a close member of one's own family.)

The third personage whose name was unlikely ever to be forgotten in the village was Henrietta Player, the artist's spinster daughter. She, too, was dead, and it was the manner of her passing which gave rise to the notoriety which attended her name. She was murdered.

Five and a half years ago, late on a hot Friday afternoon towards the end of August, sixty-two-year-old Henrietta Player was found in the bedroom of her lonely thatched cottage, brutally battered to death.

She died, it was thought, about three days before the gruesome discovery was made. (The body of the murdered woman was discovered by the police following an anonymous telephone call to the Gidding Constabulary from someone with a pronounced speech impediment.) Her murderer had never been apprehended.

Like her father, Henrietta Player cut herself off from the villagers, ignored their attempts to draw her into the community. Throughout his active working life, Edward Player had flouted just about every convention known to civilised man and had therefore been widely regarded as eccentric. Henrietta definitely had similar leanings, and everyone in the village was agreed that there was something odd, something decidedly Bohemian, about her. After her father's death in nineteen fifty-three, the front and back doors of Whitethatch Cottage were never—not at any time, night or day—locked: any stray, man or beast, was free to wander into Henrietta Player's home at will and, it was said in the village, be assured of something to eat and somewhere to sleep. With the advent of the motorway seven years ago, the number of dossers Henrietta Player tolerated in and about her cottage increased dramatically, some staying only one night before moving on, others remaining sometimes days and weeks on end.

The police were faced with an impossible task. The last person to be seen near Whitethatch Cottage around the time of the murder was a man with long greasy fair hair and waxen features, of average build, wearing faded blue jeans and thought to have been somewhere in his early to mid thirties. He was seen, and by more than one person, hanging about the cottage several days prior to the discovery of Henrietta Player's body; but James Sutherland, the veterinary surgeon who was attending Aggie (one of Mr Roper's Friesians) at the time, was the last to see him late in the afternoon of the day during which the police surgeon thought Henrietta Player died. The fair-haired man was running away from Whitethatch Cottage towards the motorway when James Sutherland saw him.

Police inquiries in the village revealed that this was not the first time that the fair-haired dosser had been to Henrietta Player's cottage. He had passed that way some three months earlier when one of the villagers, Anne Blackmore—the Vicar's wife—had actually exchanged a few words of conversation with him. Mrs Blackmore was able to tell the police that the man had a speech impediment, but this vital piece of information proved to be disappointing and of no significant help to the police in their efforts to trace him. The fair-haired dosser was never found.

Every adult, male and female, and the children of school age in the village were interviewed and over four hundred individual statements were taken, including one made by Margaret Sayer who had been holidaying on the Isle of Wight at the time of the murder.

Miss Sayer was furious, not so much about the statement she was requested to make to the police, but because she was required to give the names of two persons, either resident on the Isle of Wight or who had shared her holiday, who could verify that she had been there as and when stated by her. It made her feel a liar and a criminal and something of a fool in the eyes of her friends, especially amongst those who attended the Day Centre with her, to be treated in this fashion. Detective Chief Superintendent Sayer, the officer who had been in charge of the investigation into the murder of Henrietta Player, was her nephew, the son of one of her older brothers. (Superintendent Sayer retired from the police force following a serious heart attack which his wife, Jean, was secretly convinced had been brought about by the abnormally severe stresses and strains which had been placed upon him two years earlier when the Player murder investigation had been at its height.)

With the one exception, the villagers accepted the murder enquiries stoically and with a certain amount of sympathy for their interrogators and put it all down to Widow Roth's Stones, a similar formation of which, really no more than a handful of scattered pebbles, had been found at the foot of the bed on which the murdered woman had been discovered. The police, they assumed, thought this pointed to one of them being Miss Player's murderer. They themselves were never for one moment in any doubt who, or rather what, had killed the old lady. It was the motorway: and like the motorway, they said they had all seen it coming.

The motive for the murder was never established beyond the point of speculation. It was rumoured that Henrietta Player had kept large sums of money hidden in and about her cottage. If this were true, none was found when the police made their search of the cottage and its surrounds, which put robbery at the head of the list of possible motives. It was also thought that a painting had been stolen from the sitting-room, not because anyone had said that one was missing, but simply because there was a clean patch on the wallpaper about eighteen inches square. There were several early Player sketches and some water-colours hanging in various others parts of the cottage, all valuable, which indicated that the painting thought by the police to have been stolen from the sitting-room was probably no less valuable;

but while the art world had been alerted to watch out for any of Edward Player's works which came to light in suspicious circumstances, nothing had ever been reported back.

From time to time during the first two or three years following the murder, and as fresh scraps of evidence were turned up, the case was re-examined; but now it was generally accepted by the villagers that Henrietta Player's murderer would never be found. The murder was seldom discussed. The whole unpleasant affair was as good as forgotten. Or would have been if Cissie Keith's cousin hadn't been spending a few days with her and come face to face with Adele Herrmann—to give her her real name, the one by which Cissie Keith's cousin had known her over ten years ago. The villagers knew her simply as *Mrs Charles . . . Edwina* was thought to be her Christian name. No one was sure.

Adele Herrmann and what she had done for a living came as a terrible shock to everyone. But at least it explained what the big expensive cars were doing outside her bungalow and why that feeble-minded Forbes was so friendly with her. . . .

CHAPTER TWO

"Shook rigid he was—white as a sheet!" Margaret Sayer said for what must have been the sixth time in less than half that number of minutes.

"Cissie Keith's cousin?" Miss Sayer's nephew, David, murmured patiently, ignoring the raised eyebrows and barely concealed grin on his wife's face as she wheeled in the afternoon tea trolley.

Jean Sayer was a slim, pretty woman with a good, clear skin which had aged little in the nine and a half years since she had celebrated her fortieth birthday, despite the fact that she was frequently heard to complain, though never within her husband's hearing range, that she had put on years overnight, thanks to David's coronary.

"Well, my dear," Miss Sayer said, with heavy emphasis on the 'well', "that's what *she* calls him, but personally I think he's one of her old flames who keeps hoping he'll get his foot stuck permanently in her front door."

Miss Sayer looked past her nephew and fixed a disapproving eye on a straying branch of the lilac tree which, against her advice, Jean had planted to one side of the living-room window. Her eyes narrowed.

"They'd make a jolly good pair, those two . . . Cissie Keith and that Lionel Preston," she observed distantly. "He's as bad as she is. Got a real opinion of himself. Both ugly as they come!"

Jean Sayer poured the tea and winked at her husband behind the old lady's back.

Margaret Sayer was a terrible gossip, at times and in the manner of one who obviously feels that great age exempts one from any further obligation to observe the accepted social niceties, cruelly outspoken and quite openly and unrepentingly spiteful and vindictive. She had extraordinary ideas about most things and, no doubt influenced by the depressing world-wide economic situation presently existing, was currently holding the communists responsible for everything that went wrong, both on an international scale and to her personally.

She was a tiny woman, barely five feet tall, always bordering on overweight and determined to remain that way. Her unusually bright pink cheeks glowed with the good health which she always appeared to enjoy, but her most interesting physical feature was her hair. It was quite white now, but otherwise much as it had very nearly always been, a close-fitting skull cap of tight natural curls. When a child, her hair had hung below her shoulders and had been lovingly brushed by her mother into long ringlets. Little Margaret had hated it all, the daily brushings, the extravagant ringlets, the bright ribbons, and so much so that the day had eventually dawned when she had taken up her mother's large dressmaking scissors and had rid herself of as much of the offending matter as could be taken up in her small fingers. Her hairstyle had not altered from that day to this: anything over half an inch in length was said to get on her nerves, and if unable to get over to the hairdresser's in Gidding to have something done about it professionally, she would take matters into her own hands, irritably hacking at the tight springy curls with the same lack of restraint and regard for style and appearance she had displayed as an eight-year-old child.

Jean Sayer passed the old lady a cup of tea and smiled to herself over the possibility that Cecilia Keith with her fluffy, flaming orange hair and protruding, badly discoloured front teeth was entertaining a lover on the sly and not a member of her family as she had been leading everyone to believe. It was so bizarre a possibility that Jean Sayer was inclined to think that for once her husband's aunt was actually on to something!

Jean Sayer voiced something of what was passing through her mind as she offered a plate of freshly baked fruit scones to Miss Sayer.

"Would Cissie Keith be all that much of a catch?" she enquired.

"She's got some lolly stacked away, has that one!" Miss Sayer's brown eyes darkened under their slightly hooded, oily lids. "Colonel Billingsley thought he was getting himself nicely set up there, but that was all he knew! Cissie dropped him like a hot coal when this so-called cousin of hers turned up."

Jean Sayer frowned a little. "Colonel Billingsley? Isn't he that nice white-haired old gentleman who was calling on you a while back?"

Miss Sayer was so affronted by the suggestion that she slopped tea in her saucer.

"He did no such thing!" she exclaimed indignantly. "He fancied his chances, mind you. Thought he was on to a good thing when he found out that I had a nice little place of my own and a small private income, but I soon set his thinking straight. The only person whose feet get warm round *my* living-room fire is me! And I told him so to his face. He rapidly

lost interest after that and soon found himself someone else to sit with on the coach outings. . . ."

Miss Sayer was clearly steamed up and nowhere
near done with the gold-digging Colonel Billingsley.
In the interests of her blood pressure and the new
bottle-green Wilton which had been laid only the day
before yesterday, her nephew felt it prudent to inter-
vene.

"You were going to tell me about Cissie Keith's
cousin and Mrs Charles," he quietly reminded the old
lady, an anxious eye on the quivering hand holding
her cup and saucer.

Miss Sayer frowned at the interruption. She loathed
being side-tracked as she was warming up to her subject. For a moment she seemed confused, completely
disoriented, then her all but overflowing saucer
caught her eye, and with a nervous exclamation she
gave it her undivided attention, draining it back into
her cup. Her hands shook so badly that Jean Sayer
preferred to look elsewhere rather than watch tea
spill all over her nice new carpet.

"Lionel Preston, Cissie's cousin . . ." Miss Sayer
began at length, her undertaking safely accomplished.
She paused momentarily while she reached for another scone. "He said that Mrs Charles is Adele
Herrmann, Madame Herrmann, *the* Madame Herrmann . . . the one who murdered that old lady in
Scarborough—or was it Yarborough?—ten years ago
and got off scot-free . . . picked up her crystal ball and
vanished into the night with the poor dead woman's
jewellery."

David Sayer shook his head slowly and contrived to
look vague. A close friend—James Sutherland, the
veterinary surgeon, who attended the livestock in and
around the village—had already passed on to him a
somewhat garbled, third-hand version of Cissie

Keith's cousin's High Street encounter with Edwina Charles, and David Sayer was therefore more than just a little curious to hear his aunt's account of the same incident. However, too much obvious interest on his part would do nothing for Mrs Charles' rapidly deteriorating reputation— Not by the time his aunt had put her own interpretation on his reaction—and he knew she would be watching him keenly for one—and had spread it round the village.

"Sorry, Auntie," he said flatly. "As usual, I've absolutely no idea what you're talking about."

"Well, you should," his aunt snapped at him. "It's your job to know about such things. You interviewed Mrs *High-and-mighty* Charles when Henrietta Player was murdered: you should've spotted her real identity then, not waited for that cat's cousin to come along and do your people's job for you."

"It was neither of those places," Jean Sayer interrupted thoughtfully. "Wasn't it a much smaller seaside resort—?"

"Yes, yes—" The old lady brushed her aside impatiently. "Probably. The where isn't important. What really matters is what happened there. . . . A very rich, lonely old widow was battered to death and robbed, and the prime suspect for the crime is now living in the village under an assumed name. You of all people, David, should be the last person to need to have it pointed out to you that five or so years ago history repeated itself, and in *our* village!"

A keen light of interest shone bright in Jean Sayer's eye. "I didn't know that Mrs Charles was a clairvoyante," she said.

"None of us did, did we?" Miss Sayer sharply retorted. "She took us all in with that soft voice and those genteel refined manners of hers . . . Pretending to be something she isn't and never was!" The old lady snorted. "I've got no time for that kind. Nor for the spineless nincompoops who go in for all that fortune-telling claptrap. They've got more money than sense—a *lot* more money!" she added darkly.

"What do you mean?" Jean Sayer asked curiously.

"That's how Mrs Charles made a living for herself," Miss Sayer replied, indicating that she was waiting for her second cup of tea to be poured. "A very good living, too, Cissie's cousin says. And by all accounts she's still at it! Some of us were talking about her only the other day . . . you know, all those visitors of hers: we thought something funny was going on. Colonel Billingsley sometimes takes a walk out her way, that's if the weather's fine, and he told us . . ."

David Sayer cleared his throat and said, "How does Cissie Keith's cousin know Mrs Charles?"

There was a long pause before Miss Sayer answered. She had been pulled up short, quite deliberately, although she was far too insensitive to realise it, and it took time for her to get her train of thought to run along any track other than the one down which she had been driving it. No one hurried her.

"Lionel Preston comes from there . . . the town where the old lady was murdered," Miss Sayer finally replied to her nephew's question. "Cissie said he's lived there all his life. Mrs Charles—Adele Herrmann as he knew her—set up shop on the pier the season before Mrs Stuart died . . . Stuart was the old lady's name, the one who was murdered. Lionel Preston said it happened right in the middle of Mrs Charles' second season on the pier."

"Why was Mrs Charles suspected?" Jean Sayer asked.

"This Mrs Stuart was one of . . . I don't know what you call these stupid people—*clients,* I suppose," Miss Sayer muttered. "She saw Mrs Charles privately,

of course. Mrs Stuart was a lady of some consequence
in the town—high-born, Cissie's cousin said—not the
sort of person who would like to be seen queuing up
on the pier to consult a seaside clairvoyante. Mrs
Stuart went round to Adele Herrmann's house the
night she was murdered, and a day or so later the police found a valuable piece of Mrs Stuart's jewellery
hidden away in Adele Herrmann's bedroom. She said
Mrs Stuart had given it to her as a token of her
appreciation . . . *a diamond necklace,* if you please—
worth thousands and thousands of pounds! Cissie said
her cousin told her that it had been in the Stuart
family for hundreds of years!"

Miss Sayer paused for dramatic effect, looking with
narrowed eyes first at her nephew, then at his wife,
before continuing—

"Lionel Preston said that Mrs Charles'—Adele
Herrmann's—attitude when the police confronted her
with the necklace they'd found was almost too brazen
for words. Cool as a cucumber, she produced a piece
of paper which had been signed by the old lady, Mrs
Stuart, the night she'd been murdered, which said
that the necklace was a gift—*a gift,* mind!—and that it
was her, Mrs Stuart's, express wish that Adele
Herrmann and no one else should have it. Then just
when everyone was expecting to hear that Adele
Herrmann had been charged with the old lady's murder, up she comes with a water-tight alibi for the time
of the crime! She was entertaining a friend—the
Punch and Judy man from the sea-front! Never mind
that it was way past the hour of night when any decent self-respecting woman would consider such a
thing! Cissie's cousin told her that Adele Herrmann
came to the town in the first place because of this
Punch and Judy man who had worked the sea-front

during the summer months for quite a number of years before Adele Herrmann went there."

Miss Sayer had finished a third scone and was now breaking open a fourth. She buttered the scone with the same painstaking care afforded her toast at breakfast each morning. The butter was spread thickly and evenly right to the edges of each half. This done, she placed a large dollop of raspberry jam on the edge of her plate, a smear of which was then transferred to a small section of scone. She went on:

"Soon after the murder, the Punch and Judy man sloped off—right at the height of the season, too," she reminded her nephew with a meaningful look. "And not long after, Adele Herrmann—Mrs Charles as we know her—disappeared. Vanished!"

Miss Sayer looked from one to the other of her listeners and waited with characteristic thin-lipped impatience for some response from them.

"Where did she go—?" Jean Sayer obliged. "The village?"

This rather elementary piece of deduction was rewarded with a slow nod and a smug smile. "And now we all know why, don't we?" Miss Sayer said, the smile fading and being replaced by an indignant glare. "That fool of a man, Cyril Forbes, sent for her. He'd done all the spadework: Henrietta Player was their next victim."

David Sayer shot his aunt a startled look. "Good Lord, Auntie!" he exclaimed reprovingly. "How on earth did you arrive at that conclusion?"

"It's staring you right in the face," she said curtly. "You only have to look at him. Any fool can see that he's the Punch and Judy man."

"Did Cissie's cousin say that Mr Forbes was the man involved with Mrs Charles—Adele Herrmann?" Jean Sayer asked with a frown.

"No, he didn't," the old lady replied. Then with an airy, dismissive wave of her hand: "Cyril Forbes wouldn't be using his real name any more than Mrs Charles is, and Cissie's cousin hasn't actually seen him yet—though Cissie and I have been working on it," she assured her nephew with a thin smile. "Lionel Preston simply referred to Adele Herrmann's accomplice as 'the Punch and Judy man'. Cissie and I have put two and two together ourselves—quite a few of us have, and we've all come up with the same answer. Cyril Forbes is the Punch and Judy man; and you'll never convince me he isn't!"

"I've always rather liked Mr Forbes," Jean Sayer remarked absently. "The last of the great British eccentrics," she smiled.

"Yes, well, my dear . . ." Miss Sayer said heavily. "Eccentricity is a luxury few of us can afford these days. One needs a great deal of money to pursue Forbes' kind of folly. And no great mystery where he's acquired his—from underneath Henrietta Player's flooring-boards!"

"Malicious gossip," David Sayer said curtly. "All of it!"

"You can call it what you like," Miss Sayer said imperturbably. "But the village is buzzing with it. That's why I said I wouldn't be available for the whist-drive this afternoon, why I splashed out on the bus-fare over here to Gidding instead . . . so I could tell you to your face what's going on back there in the village. And now," she went on briskly, patting her mouth with her serviette, "you can drive me home. You'll be wanting to talk to them, Forbes and that woman . . . question them about the murders."

"I've retired, Auntie . . ." David Sayer said soberly. "In case you've forgotten. Asking questions is someone else's job now. It's no longer any concern of mine who killed Henrietta Player."

Miss Sayer nodded as though she had expected as much, and made ready to leave. "The solving of her murder is *your* responsibility, David. The village expects it of you. *I* expect it of you."

He smiled at the stern expression on her face. She had obviously suffered much embarrassment at his expense, more than he had realised.

"You'll laugh on the other side of your face, my boy, before this is over and done with," she warned him. "Why, I've got half a mind to carry out my own investigation . . . you know, like old ladies do in murder novels. That poor Miss Player," she frowned. "A nice way to die, I must say. Somebody's got to see that justice is done."

"But it won't be you," her nephew rejoined with a slow smile. "Prejudice and justice don't generally walk hand in hand. Besides, you're much too small for such a big job—you'd better think about growing a few more inches first . . . a bit more brawn?" he suggested, flexing his arm muscles at her.

"Huh!" she said. She turned to her nephew's wife. "The tea was very nice, Jean, but I thought the scones a little on the heavy side . . . too much butter, I would say. 'A light touch, a sure touch,' my mother always said; and just as important in the measuring as in the mixing . . ."

David Sayer's offer to walk his aunt to the bus stop was declined.

"I may have short legs, but I can still be there in half the time it takes you young people to think about getting off your backsides," she grimly informed him. "Anyway, the shock would be much too great for your system—it must be years since you've walked farther than your garage."

Jean Sayer went to the door with her.

"How did Mrs Charles react to Cissie Keith's cousin when she saw him?" the younger woman asked, keeping her voice low so that her husband would not hear her question. 'Fanning the fires' is what he would call it.

"Shook rigid, Cissie said she was. She nearly died of fright. Never said a word. Stood there outside the post office like somebody who's just come face to face with a ghost from the past. . . ."

"Well, what do you make of that?" Jean Sayer asked on her return to the living-room a moment or two later.

"Take no notice of her," her husband advised. "I thought they were very nice. Besides," he grinned, "you know she's always complaining about her National Health choppers, how blunt they are. . . ."

"Not the scones," she corrected him, grinning back. "I'd rather she criticised them than the new carpet, and I was sure she'd have something to say about that before she left! I was talking about that old murder case. . . ."

"You seemed remarkably well informed about it," he commented, evasively some people might have been inclined to think.

"I read all about it only a few days ago—in an article that was on the sheet of newspaper which was wrapped round the cauliflower I bought the other day. One of the Sunday papers, I think . . . they've been running a series of articles on unsolved crimes, and the Stuart murder was one of them. All the names and places had been changed to protect the identity of the people who were involved, those who are still living, but it was definitely the murder your aunt was telling us about. It was all there—the Punch and Judy man—the clairvoyante's alibi for the night the murder was committed . . ."

Jean Sayer paused and frowned thoughtfully. Then, continuing—

"Perhaps it was the way the Stuart case was presented . . . I mean, whoever wrote that article I read might've been biased and deliberately allowed his own personal feelings about the crime and the people involved to influence the reader, but I certainly got, or was given, the impression that there was a big question mark over the two of them—I couldn't help feeling that the police knew very well that the clairvoyante and the Punch and Judy man had been in collusion with one another and had murdered the old woman for her jewellery, but there'd been no way they could prove it. But I simply can't believe that the Punch and Judy man involved in that murder case was Mr Forbes—even if he is as mad as the proverbial March hare! Come to think of it," she went on after another slight pause, "he looks a bit like a hare, doesn't he?"

Her husband studied her for a moment. Then he slowly shook his head. "The old lady's right, you know . . . not that Forbes was the man involved with the clairvoyante, but about what, *who*, he reminds me of. *Mr Punch!*"

CHAPTER THREE

Ex-Detective Chief Superintendent Sayer avoided the motorway and went the long way round to the village, and simply because it was a Wednesday, and Wednesdays were to Cyril Forbes what the full moon is claimed to be to others.

Nothing depressed David Sayer more than to forget himself while speeding along the motorway and catch a glimpse of Cyril Forbes scurrying about like a nervy squirrel over the gently rolling farmland which swept down to the motorway in a wide curve. It was always roughly in the same place that Cyril Forbes was spotted and everybody knew that he was up to something out there, but what was still his secret. Shortly before his retirement, David Sayer had arranged for a discreet but none-the-less thorough search to be made of the doubtful area, but nothing had been found: not so much as a single solitary sod of earth had been anywhere other than where it belonged.

The real problem, as Superintendent Sayer and his men had seen it, had lain in not having had at least some idea of what one had been seeking out there in the fields. Guns? Bombs? Reasonable enough in this era of violence. . . . But Cyril Forbes a potential gunman with a secret cache of arms at his disposal, a lunatic bombmaker? No. Not even Cyril Forbes' loudest critic would have thought it likely that he would go to either of those extremes to achieve his own personal ends. And so the mystery remained, a war of nerves with those of the police coming off by far the worst and with more than just the one person most concerned wishing that Cyril Forbes' spirited one-man campaign to have the motorway built a hundred yards to the west of its proposed location had been successful. Unfortunately, the Department of the Environment had not shared Cyril Forbes' optimism about *The Coming* and had gone ahead and approved the plans to build the motorway over what Cyril Forbes claimed was *The Designated Spot*.

A familiar figure near The Brewery made David Sayer mutter under his breath and glance quickly at his watch, which showed that his drive through the village had been badly timed. It was eleven forty-five and his Aunt Margaret was obviously on her way to the Day Centre for her lunch ticket.

He raised a hand in quick salute as he drove past her and accelerated a little. He glanced into the rear-view mirror. By rights, she should have disappeared down the lane by the side of The Brewery, but she was still where he had first noticed her, only now she was quite motionless and obviously watching to see whether he intended to make a stop somewhere in the village or whether he would drive straight on, keeping to the road which wound its way past Edwina Charles' bungalow and would eventually bring him out on to the motorway. He sighed and wryly wondered what the topic of conversation would be on his aunt's table over lunch that day.

The last time David Sayer had called on Mrs Charles, which had been soon after the murder of Henrietta Player, five and a half years ago, the Capuchin monkey which Mrs Charles had kept as a pet had persistently removed his wallet from the inside

pocket of his jacket, the inquisitive little animal twice
successfully completing a solemn examination of the
contents of the Chief Superintendent's wallet before
it had been retrieved and apologetically returned to
its owner. David Sayer said he was sorry to hear that
the pet had since died, and hoped his relief wasn't
too apparent.

Mrs Charles responded with a grave smile and he
was instantly struck with the disquieting thought that
her deep blue eyes were capable of seeing a good deal
more than he for one would like to believe was hu-
manly possible. It was something he couldn't recall
ever having noticed about her before, and with a
fleeting twinge of regret he found himself wondering
if this hadn't somehow been a very grave error on his
part.

She was a handsome woman with beautifully
groomed, short, pale gold hair. Her face, except for
the statutory laughter lines around her eyes and
mouth, was quite smooth, which made her age difficult to determine, but her visitor was inclined to
think that she was probably somewhere in her mid- to
late-fifties.

She returned David Sayer's frankly appraising gaze
steadily and appeared to be neither surprised nor disturbed to see him. She thought he had altered considerably since their last meeting. He was slimmer
and looked better for it. He also seemed more
relaxed. The advisory capacity in which, she had
heard it said, he now served a large security organisa-
tion was obviously nowhere near as physically and
mentally taxing as his former employment.

"I miss Emma—the monkey—very much," she
confessed, showing her caller into the sitting-room,
"even if I was always threatening to send her back to
the circus if she didn't mend her ways. She really be-

longed to one of my husbands. He came from the circus, too," she smiled. "Fortunately, I didn't have to threaten him. He saved me the bother and went back of his own accord."

"Husbands?" David Sayer raised his eyebrows a little.

"Three," she owned up, smiling merrily at him with those shrewd blue eyes of hers. "Each one of whom left me that much poorer and no wiser. I'm one of these hopeless people who never seem to learn anything from past mistakes—in fact, I've often felt that I could hardly wait to plunge headlong into my next marital disaster . . . which has always, unfailingly, turned out to be more spectacular than the last."

"I should've thought that someone with your . . . er . . . *qualifications* would've been in the best possible position to have charted a smooth course through life for herself."

Mrs Charles averted her gaze from her visitor, but the smile was still there, twinkling in her eyes.

"I prefer to call it a *gift*, Superintendent," she mildly corrected him, lifting her eyes to the ornately-framed full-length photograph of a young woman on the writing bureau.

He followed her gaze. The striking-looking woman in the photograph was beautifully gowned. There was an ostrich plume in her elegant coiffure and her right hand held an exquisite fan across her breast. An Edwardian lady—David Sayer believed he was right in thinking. And unless he was very much mistaken, one who had had some connection with the theatre. . . .

"My mother had it, too," Mrs Charles went on after a thoughtful pause. "She was a remarkable woman, an exquisite creature and a talented soprano with a brilliant career in front of her until she met my father, Johann Herrmann, who sang Alfredo to her Violetta in a particularly ill-fated London production of *La Traviata*—ill-fated in the sense that Violetta's Alfredo abandoned her here in England the moment he discovered that she was pregnant. My mother was Italian, the only daughter, I understand, of a Count. Unfortunately, although the family permitted her to have her voice professionally trained, they wouldn't consent to allow her to pursue a career in the opera, and so she ran away from home, whereupon the family—her father, disowned her. It was while she was waiting my arrival that she discovered that she was clairvoyant—which was indeed fortunate for the two of us," she sighed, looking back at David Sayer. "Otherwise we would surely have starved."

"Herrmann is your maiden name."

It was a statement, not a question, and one as open and candid as the manner in which Mrs Charles was regarding him.

"That is correct," she replied. "Adele is my given name, though I am usually known, at least here in the village, by the feminine of Mr Charles'—my last husband's Christian name, Edwin. I thought a name like Edwina Charles more suited to the years I hoped to spend in quiet retirement here. Many of the old attitudes and prejudices have died out over recent years, but I wasn't sure that the distrust the English have, or had, for all that is not pure Anglo-Saxon was one of them. Until I came here, I always reverted to the use of my maiden name following my divorces. That's how Mrs Keith's cousin knows me as Adele Herrmann—I was 'twixt divorce and marriage to Mr Charles when Lionel Preston and I had occasion to meet. You would perhaps be good enough to explain that to your aunt?" She smiled, with no apparent animosity. "I am sure we can rely on her to set the record straight."

He looked embarrassed and found himself saying, "I was going to apologise and say Aunt Margaret means no harm, but I'm not at all sure that this would be true. I'm afraid she trades heavily on her age, which she seems to think gives her the licence to say what she likes. Mind you," he smiled, "I can't honestly claim to remember her any other way. My father used to say her tongue was sharper than most because she was always such a tiny little thing, and with so many older brothers, four in all, she was more or less obliged to develop an aggressive attitude towards everyone and everything in order to establish some sort of personality of her own choosing."

David Sayer frowned a little and regretted not having left things at a simple apology. Village gossip being what it was, he was sure, even though it wasn't evident from the politely interested expression of Mrs Charles' face, that she knew very well what had made Margaret Sayer the acid-tongued, embittered old woman she was today. It was hard to believe that there could actually be someone from the village who didn't know all about the bigamous marriage which Margaret Sayer's father had had discreetly 'annulled' when he'd discovered that his only daughter's newly-acquired husband already had a wife and family elsewhere. . . .

Still frowning, David Sayer went on:

"What I regret most is the gossip which Mr Preston has attached to your, Adele Herrmann's name. I'm referring, of course, to the murder ten years ago of Mrs Janet Stuart. I'm sure you're very well aware that the similarities between this murder and that of Henrietta Player not so many years ago haven't been passed over without comment in the village. . . ."

Mrs Charles was nodding her head thoughtfully. "And what about you, Superintendent? I did hear that you've retired, but you don't mind my calling you that, do you?" she queried with a quick frown.

He shook his head, and she continued:

"How do the police feel about Adele Herrmann?"

"I wouldn't know," he replied evenly, his eyes lighting momentarily on the diamond rings, six in all, which heavily adorned all but four of her fingers.

"I see," she said slowly. "Well, then . . . *you*, Superintendent: how do you regard the similarities between the two murders?"

"With interest, Mrs Charles."

She smiled. "That is very frank of you: we should get along very well with one another. I abhor hypocrisy—" She glanced at the ormolu clock on the mantelshelf and said, "I am expecting a visitor at one. I never did get to retire, not completely. I'm still consulted by those who remained faithful to me. . . ."

"The Stuart murder was bad for business?"

"I was referring to the advent of the computer," she replied gravely. "I was only one of many who were eventually forced out of business by it. It was inevitable that sooner or later someone would introduce electronics to the fortune-telling profession. However, these things come in cycles, like good and bad times, and, in my opinion, the wheel has almost completed its full revolution. Today, I am happy to be able to say, there seems to be a definite swing back to us . . . to the Tarot and the crystal ball. Now . . ." she smiled. "How can I satisfy your interest in the wicked Madame Herrmann?"

David Sayer studied her for a moment. He felt a

grudging admiration for her directness and he determined not to insult her obvious intelligence by being other than perfectly honest and straightforward with her in return. He doubted if he had any other alternative. If there were to be an interview of any kind, she was the one who would conduct it. That had become very apparent to him right from the outset.

"I would like to discuss Janet Stuart with you," he began.

She nodded briskly, as if to say, 'Yes, I thought as much.'

"My knowledge of the Stuart case is, of course, very sketchy," he went on. "And I should like to make it quite clear that the interest I have in it is strictly a personal one—"

"I understand perfectly, Superintendent," she hastened to assure him. "Please, there is no need for you to be apologetic. I appreciate how you must feel about Miss Player's murder—though I am quite sure that no one in the village felt that your task of finding her murderer was ever anything other than hopeless in the circumstances. . . . However, this current revival of interest in her murder must be particularly galling for you. And I know that if I were you, I should never feel able to rest easy until the person who murdered her was brought to justice."

CHAPTER FOUR

David Sayer nodded slowly and, at Mrs Charles' invitation, settled himself comfortably in a reproduction mid-Victorian, button-backed leather arm-chair. A copy of the *Financial Times*, he noted, was lying on the small table beside him. A pair of business-like, heavy-framed spectacles and their attractive pale blue, gold-embossed case—absurdly feminine by comparison—rested on top of the newspaper.

Mrs Charles sat down on the sofa and said, "What exactly would you like to know about Janet Stuart, Superintendent?"

"I realise that it's quite some time ago now that you knew Mrs Stuart, and that one's memory is bound not to be all that clear about an event as long in the past as her murder—"

"On the contrary," she interrupted. "I have an excellent memory where faces and places and people are concerned . . . photographic, in fact. I never forget anything or anyone. Not completely." She frowned absently, as if she and her thoughts were suddenly drawn elsewhere. She came back to him with a quick, somewhat apologetic smile. "A simple matter of training and self-discipline," she explained. "There is, I regret to say, nothing psychic or supernatural about my powers of recollection. . . ." She hesitated before continuing, and her face took on a vaguely concerned look. "I think I ought to point out to you, here and now, Superintendent, that Janet Stuart and I were never closely acquainted with one another. I knew her only very sightly—"

Mrs Charles fell silent (rather abruptly, David Sayer considered) and looked at him expectantly. He studied her thoughtfully. She had been going to continue, to add something else, but she had thought better of it, and he wondered why. After a long moment, he nodded and because he felt it was probably required of him, verbally expressed his acceptance of her claim that the relationship which had existed between her and the murdered woman had not been an intimate one. He then went on:

"Just how long had Mrs Stuart been coming to see you before she died?"

"Only a very short time—a month . . . five or six weeks at the most. She made her second visit to see me on the night she was murdered."

"I understand that she was consulting you about the future. Did she have some cause for concern about what lay ahead of her, some specific reason for wanting to know her fate in advance?"

"Of course—" Mrs Charles seemed mildly surprised by the question. "There's always a reason, Superintendent. However, in Mrs Stuart's case, it wasn't the one given me." She paused and gazed momentarily out of the window. Looking back at him, she continued:

"Some people tackle their problems head on and openly: many more prefer the indirect, devious approach. . . . Mrs Stuart was one such person. She never felt able to come right out and tell me what was troubling her."

"But you surely had some idea of what was really

on her mind?" His raised eyebrows emphasised the element of surprise in his voice.

Again she hesitated. "If you want a black-and-white answer to that question," she eventually replied, "then I'm afraid I can't give you one. I never progressed beyond an awareness that Mrs Stuart was deliberately holding something back from me."

"Am I to take this as a confession of fraudulence?" he enquired coolly.

"Indeed no—nor was it an admission of impotence," she smiled. "Let me explain how it was between Mrs Stuart and me. . . . Janet Stuart's first visit to see me was arranged in what I can only describe as most extraordinary cloak-and-dagger secrecy, over a period of two weeks, by means of unsigned notes acquainting me with her urgent need to see me. No name was ever mentioned, not at that juncture. The notes were pushed under the door to my booth on the pier—" She raised her eyebrows interrogatively and he indicated that he was aware that that had been how she had once spent her summers. She then went on:

"I was never quick enough to see who left them and, in any event, it was the height of the summer season: the pier was packed with holidaymakers. It could've been anybody, even youngsters playing a practical joke on me," she smiled gravely. "Nevertheless, the notes proved to be quite genuine, for in time the person who had written them, Janet Stuart, and I met. She came to my home late one evening, greatly agitated and very obviously frightened of something, or someone, and largely incoherent as a result of that fear. She was interested only in a reading of the Tarot, and this I did for her. . . . I provide a fully comprehensive fortune-telling service which includes a reading of the palm, the Tarot and the crystal ball," she paused to explain. "But Mrs Stuart was adamant that the Tarot was all that she had time for that night. However, from my point of view I was far from satisfied with the reading I gave her—the poor woman's extreme state of nervous anxiety thwarted every attempt I made to probe too deeply into her future.

"The first card, Superintendent— We clairvoyantes all have our own little idiosyncrasies, our own *modus operandi,* so to speak, and I doubt if any two of us would work in exactly the same fashion. But, for me, the first card in a reading of the Tarot is always the most interesting and the key which immediately turns the lock on the door to the whole picture. And yet in this instance," she frowned reflectively, "the lock didn't seem to want to be turned. The first card and almost every card thereafter went no further than to confirm what I already knew . . . that the seeker, Mrs Stuart, was an extremely anxious woman and that she was intensely afraid of something. Possibly someone. I could divine little else—that is, until I turned up an inverted symbolic card from the Major Arcana, card number thirteen. The seven of clubs from the Minor Arcana was its reinforcing card."

David Sayer told himself that he was imagining things, but for a moment there it looked very much to him as though a shadow crossed Mrs Charles' face.

"I'm not familiar with the Tarot, Mrs Charles: perhaps you would be good enough to explain the significance of those two cards?" he asked, a trifle curtly. A request of this nature seemed to him not only to signify his approval of the practice of fortune-telling, but to indicate that he acknowledged its validity. And nothing could have been further from the truth!

She smiled as if aware of his conflict and amused by it. "Certainly . . ." she said pleasantly, getting up.

"It would be my pleasure." She continued to talk as she crossed to the writing bureau and removed something from it.

"The seventy-eight cards of the Tarot are divided into two parts or packs known as the Major Arcana and the Minor, or Lesser, Arcana. Some clairvoyantes use only the twenty-two symbolic cards of the Major Arcana. The more skilled prefer to use the combined Arcana. My predictions are always from a reading of the full deck."

She was back on the sofa, regarding him earnestly. "Now," she went on, "to return to the two cards which I mentioned earlier on. Card number thirteen in the Major Arcana, a symbolic card, is DEATH and was, as I said, inverted—or, in other words, placed upside down . . . an act which in itself has great significance and bearing on the reader's, my, interpretation of this card."

She had leaned forward and placed a picture card on the low occasional table over which she and her visitor faced one another. The card bore the Roman numerals for thirteen. She looked up. "This card, not necessarily on its own but when read in conjunction with the cards surrounding it, as on that particular night, clearly predicted the death of the seeker, Mrs Stuart, and also warned that the effects of her death would continue far beyond the grave in acts of very great evil. The seven of clubs, one of the fifty-six cards in the Minor Arcana, clarified the manner in which Mrs Stuart would die."

Very deliberately, Mrs Charles placed the seven of clubs directly beneath the inverted symbolic card and then looked up again. "I could see that death when it came to Janet Stuart, Superintendent, was going to be violent, unnatural."

David Sayer left his chair and came round to her

side of the table and gazed down at the two cards. Predictably, DEATH was depicted by the Grim Reaper, a curiously lissome skeleton, and was, David Sayer thought, a most unpleasant-looking card and one which left him feeling faintly disturbed even though he would never allow that the Tarot was anything other than a party game, a stupidly dangerous one at that.

"How many other cards were there?" he asked, returning to his chair.

"Twenty-two. It was a twenty-four card spread. The first twelve cards, included in which was the symbolic card from the Major Arcana, were the important ones: those which followed simply enabled me to give a more penetrating analysis of the meanings of the other more important cards. The second twelve cards can modify, confirm or in some way lend added weight and significance to the first twelve. They can also weaken or strengthen, as was the case with Mrs Stuart's reading where the seven of clubs reinforced the prediction of death."

She hesitated: then, frowning a little—

"You will appreciate that for ease of understanding, I have deliberately over-simplified the reading I gave Mrs Stuart that night and picked out only the salient points, those which I feel will be of the most interest to you. It was, as I've already indicated, a particularly difficult and complicated reading."

"Did you tell Mrs Stuart all that you've just told me?" he enquired.

"Mrs. Stuart knew her life was in peril and she also knew the reason why, Superintendent," she replied gravely. "Confirmation of her darkest fears was not why she had come to me. I asked her to see me again and urged her in the meanwhile to consider allowing me to look in the crystal for her. It was my hope—in fact, looking back, I now think that I knew for sure—that if she came back to see me in time, the crystal would reveal the exact nature, the true source of her fear. Once I knew what or who she was afraid of, I could help her. . . ."

"Did she agree to see you again?"

"No, not really. She said she wasn't sure that it would be possible for her to come again, but she promised me that she would try. Several weeks went by before I heard from her again. She left another note at my booth to say that she would be around to my home to see me that same night; but she never came. Then the night she was murdered, she suddenly reappeared on my doorstep, quite unexpectedly, and begged to be allowed to come inside and see me. I was very disturbed by her appearance: she looked ill, dreadfully ill; and yet she was somehow much calmer . . . resigned, I felt, to whatever fate had in store for her. I took her into my living-room and again read the Tarot. Then I looked in the crystal. . . ."

"And?" Despite himself, David Sayer found that he was intensely interested to hear what the crystal ball had revealed to her.

She smiled a little. "I saw myself," she said.

"I don't understand. . . ." He spoke slowly and looked puzzled. "I thought it was considered bad form for a fortune-teller, someone like you, to look into the future for herself."

She was still smiling. "It wasn't my future I was looking into, Superintendent: Mrs Stuart was the seeker, not I. You see, Janet Stuart had no future beyond that night. And whatever evil had attached to her was now attached to me. Around my neck, the neck of the spectre I saw in the crystal that night, was a necklace . . . one I had never seen before. That

was a Saturday night, and on the following Monday
morning the postman delivered a long brown envelope, the post-date on which was that of the day before, the Sunday . . . though the letter had almost
surely been posted late the previous night after the
collections were over for the day. Inside the envelope
was a brief note from Janet Stuart thanking me for
having seen her again and enclosing a necklace which
I immediately recognised as being the one I had seen
in the crystal. She said the necklace was hers and
asked me to accept it in payment for the two visits
she had made to my home and for the inconvenience
and nuisance which she seemed to think she had
caused me. I had no idea of the value of the necklace
until a short while later when the police arrived to
question me about the poor soul's murder. I won't
pretend that it had ever been other than obvious to
me that Mrs Stuart had been quite well-to-do, but I
naturally assumed that the necklace was paste, an excellent reproduction, instead of which I was amazed
to learn that the stones were real diamonds."

David Sayer glanced at Mrs Charles' heavily-ringed
fingers and wondered if it were likely that a woman
with her obvious liking for valuable gems would
make such a mistake. He doubted it.

"May I ask what became of the necklace?"

"You may," she smiled. "It is still in my possession.
There was a terrible to-do about it, of course. The executor of Mrs Stuart's estate was most put out when I
refused to hand it over—apparently it was the last
item of real value she had left. For a number of years
she'd been steadily selling off bits and pieces of her
other jewellery and generally living most imprudently
off capital."

"Didn't you feel that you had a moral obligation to
her heirs to let them have the necklace?" he

enquired. "You surely won't deny that it was an unusually high fee for someone to be expected to pay for two visits to a clairvoyante?"

The blue eyes lost most of their former warmth and friendliness, and her expression became quite severe.

"The only moral obligation I have ever had in regard to the gift of that necklace has been to respect Mrs Stuart's wishes. Don't you see? It was her way of telling me what she feared; and I was convinced that if I kept the necklace, I would uncover the truth, discover who murdered her—even though the wisest course of action I could've taken, in view of the evil and danger which I believed to be attached to the necklace and myself as its new owner, would've been to dispose of it as quickly as possible."

David Sayer's eyes were wide with disbelief. Did the woman take him for a fool? She didn't really expect him to swallow a story like that did she? His expression hardened. He had met some pretty brazen villains in his time, but this audacious woman could have taught all of them a thing or two.

"I'd say a period of ten years was a fair enough length of time for you to have come up with some answers," he said curtly. "Always assuming that you weren't mistaken about all this evil and danger you keep referring to," he finished dryly.

Mrs Charles fixed her gaze on him. "I am never mistaken, Superintendent," she said evenly. "I have never once made a prediction like the one from my first reading of the Tarot for Mrs Stuart that has not later come to pass. However, I do agree with you that one would've thought that the passage of so many years should have provided some sort of answer to the riddle of the poor woman's death. But unfortunately I'm no wiser now than I was when she died."

"I am curious to know what brought you here to this village, Mrs Charles?" he asked, unable to keep the impatience he now felt with her out of his voice. "There are so many similar villages dotted round the countryside. Why this one?"

She hesitated before replying.

"The Punch and Judy man sent for me— Isn't that what they are saying in the village?" she asked.

"Is it true?"

There was a closed expression on Mrs Charles' face, and for an uncomfortable moment David Sayer thought she was going to ignore the question and suggest, perhaps, that he should leave. He was wondering how best to recover the situation when she abruptly turned her head away and said, "No—I came here of my own accord."

"But everyone is right in thinking that the person generally referred to in the Stuart murder enquiry as 'the Punch and Judy man' is here in the village?" David Sayer leaned forward a little in his chair. "Is that man Cyril Forbes?"

"Yes. Which brings us to your next question, does it not, Superintendent?" she asked coolly, looking directly back at him. "One on the matter of coincidence . . . that Cyril Forbes should have been my alibi for the Stuart murder ten years ago and, as fate would have it, was also with me—as you already know—some five or so years later throughout most of the afternoon and evening of the day during which Henrietta Player was murdered. A coincidence, Superintendent, but one which I am sure you'll agree now places Cyril Forbes and me in a very bad light."

"In view of the close similarities between the two crimes, I am bound to say yes, it certainly does, Mrs Charles—and will certainly appear that way to the police over in Gidding, should they feel that all this gossip that's apparently been going around the village over the past few days warrants a further look at the Player murder."

The blue eyes had widened. "What similarities would those be, Superintendent?"

"Both murder victims were elderly, relatively defenceless and friendless; one was by your own admission comfortably fixed financially, the other reputed to have kept large sums of money hidden in her cottage; both were brutally attacked in practically the same fashion . . . battered to death, one with a carved onyx book-end and the other with the heavy brass base on a tablelamp."

"Yes?" she said, a strange somehow expectant look on her face.

His eyebrows rose interrogatively. "I'm sorry—?"

The expectant look faded from Mrs Charles' face and she became thoughtful, distant. Then she shook her head quickly and said, "It's nothing—"

"No . . ." he said firmly. "You expected me to mention something else, didn't you? What was it you thought I was going to say, Mrs Charles?"

"I thought you were going to tell me that both crimes were committed by a woman," she admitted hesitantly.

"Now what has led you to suppose that I'd make a statement like that?" he asked evenly.

She smiled. "Oh, I know everyone in the village said that the fair-haired man who came from the motorway killed Henrietta Player, but when you came here to my home soon after she was murdered and talked to me about her, I knew that you had made up your mind that the person you sought for the crime was a woman."

David Sayer met her smiling gaze stoically. She was right, of course. She had read his mind then just as

clearly and surely as she had today. There could be
no other explanation: he had discussed with no one,
not even with his wife, Jean, his own personal belief
that despite all the other overwhelming evidence
against the fair-haired vagrant who was still actually
wanted by the police in connection with the crime,
Henrietta Player had been murdered by a woman.

CHAPTER FIVE

Mrs Charles sat quite still and listened to David Sayer drive away from her bungalow. The concern she felt did not show on her face, which was perfectly serene. Only the colour of her eyes betrayed that all was not well behind them: they darkened noticeably with the increasing intensity of her thoughts. . . .

The Stuart murder had been different. There had been no precedent to which the police and the Miss Sayers of this world could refer. But with the Player murder— To quote a particularly apt phrase, she thought wryly, she was caught like a rat in a trap. Unless— The smooth brow was disturbed by a thoughtful frown. Yes . . . it was her only hope, the only sensible thing to do. She mulled over the plan of action which had hazily formed itself in her mind. First things first, she decided. The *Player*. . . . She would have to try and get it back.

She quickly left the sofa and went into the hall and took down her flowing scarlet wool cloak from the coatstand. A matching, black tasselled scarf was hastily wound round her throat. Then she remembered, and she grumbled a little under her breath. It was Wednesday. Cyril would be *incommunicado!* It would be a waste of time thinking about him until to-morrow—*late* tomorrow, she amended, removing her cloak and scarf. The older he got, the longer his de-hypnotisation processes seemed to take to work!

Returning to the sitting-room, she went over to the writing bureau and searched out a sheet of plain notepaper. Then she drew up a chair and sat down and began to write—

> Private collector will pay good prices for early Edward Player water-colours, etc. Particularly interested in *The Brewery*. All transactions handled in strictest confidence. Tel:

She paused and made a little drumming sound on the note-paper with her left forefinger. She couldn't put down her telephone number, of course. Or Cyril's. Someone in the village might see the ad. She would have to use someone else's . . . someone she could rely on not to ask awkward questions, and preferably someone who was on the London exchange. Elaina Petrovic, she finally decided. She would phone her around seven this evening and sound her out. She looked across at the mantelshelf and listened thoughtfully to the clock as it quietly ticked away the seconds. Seven was perhaps a little early. . . . She would hate to interrupt Elaina while she was in the middle of reading someone's horoscope. To be on the safe side, she would leave it until nine o'clock to ring her. She didn't really think for a moment that Elaina Petrovic, with whom she had at one time—when they had both been very young—shared digs and some very happy times, would raise any objections to her proposal, but she was quite sure that Cyril Forbes would. . . .

She smiled and let her thoughts dwell momentarily on the narrow escape that Cyril Forbes had once had from the marital clutches of the formidable 18-

stone Oxford Street astrologist and her daughter, Tanya, both of whom had been very determined to draw him into their intimate family circle. He had been just as determined to stay outside of it and, fortunately for him, during the ensuing stalemate Elaina Petrovic had received and accepted a proposal of marriage from a wealthy Jersey gentleman whose horoscope she read annually, one of the clients who had been with her for so many years that he qualified for the 'special rate.' Two years had seen Elaina Petrovic a widow again which, to the best of Mrs Charles' knowledge, was her present marital status.

No, Mrs Charles mused wryly, provisionally adding her friend's telephone number to the advertisement that she had just drafted out, Cyril would be most unhappy about involving Elaina in her little scheme: he would say it was tempting fate, asking for trouble.

Still smiling a little, Mrs Charles spent the next few minutes reading through the draft advertisement and making out a list of London daily newspapers. She went over the list several times before she was completely satisfied with it; then she nodded her head and murmured, "Yes, that should do it."

She sat back quietly to think. Anne Blackmore was next. Should she phone first to say she was coming or should she forget the proprieties and simply just arrive? Surprise, they said, was always the best weapon of attack. . . . Mrs Charles abruptly got up and left the room.

David Sayer had driven only a short distance from her small neat bungalow before drawing into the side of the road and taking out his pipe. Acting on the insistent advice of his doctor, he had recently switched from cigarettes to this apparently less risky form of smoking which now showed every promise of curing him of the habit altogether. He kept telling himself it was early days yet, but the evidence of his continuing inability to keep the pipe alight was steadily mounting. He was on his seventh match—he had got into the habit of keeping the score of spent matches, with twenty the record to date—when Mrs Charles seemed to swirl down on him from out of nowhere like a great thick scarlet mist. She gave him such a fright that he dropped the lighted match on to his lap and singed his trousers.

"You really must let me show you how to smoke a pipe some day, Superintendent," she gaily offered. "There's quite an art to it, you know. My first husband was an inveterate pipe smoker and for a time held the world record for keeping a pipe alight for the longest period of time. Of course, he had more than the average amount of practice at it," she smiled. "It was certainly all I ever saw him do!"

"Not a cancelled appointment, I hope?" David Sayer remarked, pointedly noting that it was just after one fifteen.

The direct blue eyes met his and twinkled a little. "Oh, you mean my appointment at one?" she smiled. "You must forgive me, Superintendent. Force of habit, I'm afraid. It's an old ruse of mine, one I use to ensure that no one ever overstays their welcome. You'd be surprised how many of my visitors never know when it's time to go home."

In the blinking of an eyelid she was gone, off down the road, the scarlet cloak and the tails of her scarf flowing majestically behind her. *Little Red Riding Hood,* he smiled to himself, following her progress with an interested eye. He wondered what was in the wicker shopping-basket she was carrying. Goodies of some kind, he felt sure. She wouldn't have bothered to cover up her library books with a best damask table-napkin!

He sighed and knocked out his pipe in the ash-tray;
then he started up the engine and drove on. He was
just in time to see Mrs Charles veer abruptly to her
left and disappear through the little side-gate to the
vicarage. Now that *was* interesting, he thought. He
turned right at The Brewery and drove slowly past
the Day Centre, then on through the rest of the quiet
village back towards Gidding.

Inside the Day Centre, the hot mid-day meal that
had been consumed there a short while earlier was
now being quietly and contentedly digested by its
fifty-four participants, the average age of whom was
seventy-one years, with ladies outnumbering gentlemen by eight to one.

The tables had been cleared. Cissie Keith and another woman were out in the kitchen doing the washing up—'*Abject crawling,*' Margaret Sayer was heard
to mutter as the two women had volunteered for the
chore. It was Joyce Gee's job to do the dishes, washing
and wiping up, and she was paid good money by the
Council to get on with it and not to sit around smoking and waiting for a pair of silly cats like Cissie
Keith and Florrie Fenton to offer to do it for her—an
opinion loudly voiced by Miss Sayer whenever anyone
(Cissie Keith and Florrie Fenton more often than
not) showed any inclination to help out in the
kitchen.

The erring Mrs Gee was sitting with Miss Marsden,
the cheerful, good-natured middle-aged woman who
ran the Day Centre for the local authority, and Miss
Sayer, all three of whom were engaged in conversation with Anne Blackmore, who had called round to
finalise arrangements for the following afternoon
when she was giving a cream tea to show her own
personal appreciation of the contribution which had
been made by the ladies and gentlemen of the Day

Centre towards the raising of funds for a new steeple for the church. As a special treat, Miss Marsden had organised a visit to a stately home which was to be spread over the greater part of the day, with the cream tea at the vicarage rounding out what everyone eagerly anticipated would be a very pleasant day's outing.

Mrs Blackmore had arrived at the Day Centre shortly before lunch-time, intending to stay only a few minutes, but a surplus of food occasioned by the unexpected absence of two regulars had resulted in an invitation to share the mid-day meal, which she had readily accepted as a welcome alternative to eating alone. The Vicar was over in Gidding on church business and she was not expecting him back much before three thirty.

The conversation among the four women moved on from the visit that the Day Centre had recently made to see the Lions of Longleat to menus: shepherd's pie and two veg., Mrs Gee told Mrs Blackmore, was always the menu for Wednesday.

With wildly exaggerated movements of her right hand, Miss Sayer fanned away the cigarette smoke which Mrs Gee persistently exhaled in her direction. *Lazy cat!* Miss Sayer fumed to herself. Then through the fug, she spotted Cissie Keith, Florrie Fenton having been left to finish off the wiping down on her own. Cissie Keith appeared to be making up her mind whether or not she should join Miss Marsden and the others.

"Wait for it," Miss Sayer hissed, her hand remaining momentarily stationary in mid-air. "I think . . . yes, here comes Cissie. It's about time we all heard how bad her back is today."

"Has she had some sort of accident to it?" Mrs Blackmore enquired in a conspiratorial whisper.

"*No*. The coach outing . . ." Miss Sayer replied under her breath. "Cissie Keith, Agnes Twopenny and Florrie Fenton always develop back trouble the day before we're due to go on a coach outing—so that they can sit near the driver. Cissie would never have bothered to turn up today if it hadn't been for tomorrow's outing: we haven't seen anything of her down here for days, not since that cousin of hers arrived. She only wants to make sure that she gets the two of them the best seats up the front of the coach."

"Oh." Mrs Blackmore nodded gravely and glanced at Miss Marsden, who raised her eyebrows a fraction in response.

Mrs Keith was an overdressed, fussy-looking woman with large protruding front teeth which had shaped her mouth into a permanent simpering half-smile. A dark green cloche-hat covered all but a wispy bang of her quite extraordinary bright orange hair. She groaned a little as she lowered her apparently painful lumbar region into a vacant chair near Miss Marsden's.

"Bad back, Cissie dear?" Miss Sayer enquired bitingly. "Perhaps you should have a day or two in bed until it gets better?"

"Oh, no, I couldn't do that," Cissie Keith assured her. "I'm so looking forward to our outing tomorrow. So is Lionel," she beamed at Miss Marsden. "It's very good of you to let him come, too. He wouldn't know what to do with himself with me out all day."

"I should've thought he'd be able to keep himself very well occupied in that garden of yours," Miss Sayer said sharply. She glared at Mrs Keith for a moment, then looked away in disgust. The outing was *supposed* to be a special treat for the people who had worked so hard for the new steeple. . . . What had Lionel Preston done towards it? Or Cissie for that matter . . . and one or two other people that she could mention whose names were down to go? Nothing! It was no use crying off because one was all fingers and thumbs where needlework was concerned. Old Mrs Hatchard's hands were crippled with arthritis, but that hadn't stopped her from doing her little bit. The toilet-roll covers that she had knitted had been so popular that every single one of them had been sold before they had even come off the needles!

Miss Sayer glowered at Mrs Keith and no one could have been in any doubt about what she was thinking . . . Cissie and her cousin had no right to go tomorrow, no right at all!

Mrs Blackmore stood up as they were joined by a sixth person, someone else with back troubles, and Miss Marsden went with her to the door, abandoning poor Mrs Fenton and her aches and pains at the mercy of Miss Sayer's acid tongue.

CHAPTER SIX

Mrs Blackmore found the basket on the front door-step. In it were six pots of home-made strawberry jam, all neatly labelled, and an accompanying note from Mrs Charles. "Of all people!" Mrs Blackmore marvelled to her husband when he returned from Gidding later that afternoon. She went on:

"Mrs Charles said she'd heard about the cream tea that I'm putting on for the folk from the Day Centre tomorrow afternoon and said she'd be very pleased if I would serve them her jam. . . ."

Frank Blackmore looked amazed. "*Edwina Charles* made that jam?"

"So she said in the note."

The pots of jam were lined up on the scrubbed pine kitchen-table and the Blackmores gazed at them in almost revered silence.

"Can't imagine it myself," Mr Blackmore confessed at length.

"No," his wife agreed. "It takes some imagining, doesn't it? I wonder—?" She eyed him speculatively. "Do you think she takes them off . . . all those rings . . . while she's working in the kitchen?"

"I very much doubt it," he replied after giving the matter some thought. "It would be like 'streaking' to her, wouldn't it? All that naked flesh parading itself before her eyes!"

Mrs Blackmore laughed. "Vulgar, aren't they? Must be worth a small fortune. Wouldn't it be nice if one of the diamonds came out of its setting and found its way into a pot of her jam?" she grinned.

"Perhaps we should forget about your little tea-party and keep the jam for ourselves—just in case?" he grinned back. "Never mind the steeple: we could afford a whole new church from the proceeds of the sale of one of those diamonds of hers!"

They both laughed; then, after another small silence, Mrs Blackmore said:

"I've just been thinking, Frank. The summer fete . . . I wonder if Mrs Charles would run a fortune-telling stall for us? Remember the year Mrs Hatchard dressed up as a gypsy and read palms? She never got a moment's peace all afternoon: there were still people waiting to have their fortunes told when we started to take down her tent that night; and Mrs Hatchard said that some people actually came round to her home the next day to ask her to read their palms. She even had people from Gidding phoning her! I'm sure it would be tremendously popular with everyone if we did something along those lines again this year. I wonder if Mrs Charles has got a crystal ball?" She frowned thoughtfully. "We could ask her to bring it along and . . ."

Her husband was shaking his head. "The villagers wouldn't like it, Anne," he said. "Not in the circumstances. It would be in very bad taste. They now regard Miss Player as having been very much one of themselves, which means that for the time being, they'll be extremely sensitive about Mrs Charles. A proposal like the one that you've just made would be taken as a slight, an affront to all that's decent and proper. You know how quickly they close ranks when they think that one of their own has suffered a terrible wrong."

She nodded slowly. "You're right: I should've known better. . . . The Day Centre was absolutely buzzing with gossip about Mrs Charles over lunch today. The poor woman's ears must've been on fire! Miss Sayer said that David went over to see Mrs Charles some time this morning."

He raised his eyebrows a little in interest. "What for?"

"Miss Sayer didn't say—" She hesitated. Then: "As a matter of fact, I don't think she was asked why: everyone seemed more interested in what she was saying about Cyril Forbes. She seems to think he's this Punch and Judy man that everyone's talking about. You've got to admit it is possible," she frowned. "Mr Forbes is the only real friend that Mrs Charles has in the village—though that's no one's fault but her own. She could've been a bit more forthcoming. . . ."

"Anne," her husband said, his tone slightly reproving.

She wrinkled her nose at him. She was an attractive, titian-haired woman, in her late thirties, always very fashionably dressed. Much too sophisticated for a country parson's wife, was the general consensus of opinion when she and her husband first came to St Stephen's eight years ago. Frank Blackmore was considerably less clothes conscious. His shapeless, well-patched, worn look was what had prompted the remark from Margaret Sayer, less than a month after Frank Blackmore had taken up his new appointment and within Mrs Blackmore's hearing, that it was very obvious where the economies were effected in his household.

"Perhaps the gift of the jam means that Mrs

Charles has seen the error in her ways?" Mrs Blackmore suggested with a shrug. "Odd though that she should pick now, this particular point in time, to want to make amends. Some people might be moved to wonder if she has an ulterior motive— And don't bother to glare at me," she cautioned her husband with a defiant toss of her titian head. "I'm not going to be a hypocrite and pretend it hasn't occurred to me that she needs a friend now more than ever before. . . . Well, never let it be said that I wouldn't meet someone half-way. I'll pop round tomorrow—no, Friday—and thank her for the jam, and we'll see where that leads us."

They were silent for a moment or two, and then he eyed her curiously. "Surely the mere fact that Mrs Keith hasn't confirmed the rumour about Mr Forbes puts paid to it. It is Cissie Keith and her cousin— what's the man's name?" he frowned. "Prescott? *Pres*—something—we have to thank for this overwhelming display of Christian charity that we are currently being subjected to, isn't it?"

She said it was, and then continued:

"Mrs Keith said her cousin couldn't remember the name of the man. Apparently it was obscured by the fact that he earned a living putting on Punch and Judy shows at the seaside: the Press caught on to it and that was the finish of his name. He was never called anything else but 'the Punch and Judy man', and Mrs Keith said that her cousin seemed to recall that he was related to Mrs Charles in some way or another. Poor Miss Sayer," she smiled. "You should've seen her face when she heard that: it dropped a mile. I think she rather liked the idea that Mrs Charles was in the habit of keeping lovers, not only *in* the bed but under it and hanging up in the wardrobes, too."

There was a small thoughtful pause. Then Anne Blackmore put their identical thoughts into words.

"An odd business," she remarked, wrinkling her nose a little.

"Very," he agreed.

"Do you think there could be something in what they're saying?" she asked. "Gossip it might be, but there's no denying that there are some remarkable co-incidences between the two murders."

"I daresay that's why David came over today—though I can't understand why it should've been him and not someone from the Gidding Constabulary . . . unless the people over there want to play down the whole affair and don't want their enquiries to look too official . . . you know, in case there's nothing in all this talk that's going round. It could explain his visit. One way or another, something certainly has to be done about the gossip," Frank Blackmore frowned. "And fairly quickly, too. The poor woman can't carry on here with such a big shadow of suspicion hanging over her head. Life would be quite intolerable for her."

"I think she'll do what she did before—pack her bags and disappear."

"You know you've pointed out a very curious anomaly there, Anne," he said musingly. "Isn't Mrs Charles supposed to have left, vanished, within a few days of having been exonerated by the police of any connection with that other murder? Henrietta Player was murdered over five years ago. If Mrs Charles killed her, why didn't she leave as soon as the coast was clear?"

"Nobody suspected her," she reminded him. "She was the prime suspect the other time . . . at least, that's what they're saying in the village. They're also saying that the murdered woman—I think I can remember someone mentioning that she was a Mrs Stuart—consulted Mrs Charles about the future."

"Well, Miss Player certainly didn't," he said flatly.

"How do you know? Why, that time I saw Mrs Charles over at Miss Player's cottage she could've been calling on her for that very purpose!"

"When was that?" he asked, surprised. "I don't remember your saying that you'd seen Mrs Charles over there."

She widened her eyes a little. "I don't think I would've recalled her visit myself if it hadn't been for the strawberry jam. It was Mrs Charles' shopping-basket—the one that she left with the jam—that brought it back to me. And don't get too far ahead of me," she frowned in response to the quickening look of interest in her husband's eye. "It was months and months—it could've even been as much as a year—before Miss Player was murdered." She hesitated and was momentarily lost in thought. Then, very slowly, she went on:

"No, I could be wrong there: it was this time of year. I remember now . . . it was a bitterly cold day." She gave her husband a long hard look. "Perhaps it wasn't as far back as I thought: it might've been only a few months before Miss Player's death. She died during summer—in August, wasn't it?—but this was winter and Mrs Charles was wearing her cloak . . . not the one that she's got now, the other one, the purple-and-black tartan. Mrs Charles had the basket with her that day. It's stuck in my mind because it's exactly like the one in the picture story-book about Little Red Riding Hood that I used to have when I was a child. . . . I was coming away from Miss Player's cottage—you know, after one of my many futile attempts to draw her into the community—and I passed Mrs Charles on the road."

"Edwina Charles was visiting Henrietta Player?"

Frank Blackmore looked as incredulous as he sounded.

"Yes. I didn't think so at first: I naturally thought that Mrs Charles was on her way to see Mr Forbes, but when I looked back, Miss Player was standing at the door talking to her; and then a few moments later, they both went inside. . . ." She paused thoughtfully. "It's funny how things come back to you . . . the way something like Mrs Charles' *Little Red Riding Hood* basket can bring back a whole host of little memories that might otherwise have never been recalled to mind."

"Did you tell the police about this when they talked to you?"

"No—I never gave it a thought; and anyway, the police—everyone—seemed so sure that Miss Player had been murdered by that nasty man with the speech defect. Though as the only person from the village, aside from Miss Player, that is, who actually spoke to him, it's always bothered me that he rang the police and told them she was dead. . . . I know nobody knows for sure that it was him, but . . . well . . . who else could it have been? It had to be the same man, the one I spoke to; and that's always seemed a bit odd to me. There was something peculiar about him, sinister almost, but I wouldn't have said he was . . . *kinky*—the sort of mentally deranged person who kills somebody and then wants the satisfaction of telling the police all about it himself. And," she frowned, "that's what her killer had to be . . . *deranged*. An absolute madman. Or woman," she added soberly.

"You don't think he murdered her?"

"I don't know . . . I've got my doubts . . . I think I've always had them. But then again," she sighed, "the gossip about Mrs Charles had probably had something to do with that. Some of it is certainly very convincing and it would be useless to try and pretend that one hasn't been a teeny bit influenced by it."

"I wonder if the police ever found out that she had been friendly with Miss Player?" he mused out loud.

"They . . . David Sayer, I think, went to see her, didn't he?"

"That doesn't mean anything: the police saw nearly everyone in the whole village, seventy per cent of whom wouldn't have so much as said 'good morning' or 'good afternoon' to Miss Player in all the time that she lived amongst them. If you ask me, I think David went to see Mrs Charles because her bungalow, like Forbes' place, lies near the motorway and there was therefore a possibility that she might've seen someone, your man with the speech defect, walking along the road."

"Mr Forbes might have seen him, but not Mrs Charles. Miss Player's cottage lies between Mr Forbes' house and Mrs Charles' bungalow," she reminded him. "Mrs Charles would only have seen someone who was travelling on foot from the motorway if that person walked on into the village after stopping at Miss Player's cottage . . . and that was something Miss Player's visitors never did: her cottage was the nearest any of them ever seemed to come to the village proper."

He nodded thoughtfully.

"What a sad way for anyone to die," she went on, sighing a little. "I mean to be so alone and friendless, nobody knowing or caring if you were alive or dead, and worse, actually wanting it that way!"

They were quiet for a very long moment.

"She was a strange woman," Anne Blackmore said at length. "Miss Player, I mean. . . ."

"Yes," her husband sighed. "It was very sad."

CHAPTER SEVEN

Mrs Charles peered in turn into the three handleless mugs which were lined up along the window-ledge over the kitchen sink. The good quarter-inch thick fur coat of bluish-grey mould that was covering the contents of the third mug made her wince.

"And what gastronomic horror, may I ask, is this?" She fixed Cyril Forbes with a stern eye. "You've been keeping gravy left-overs again, haven't you?"

There was a slight glaze to Cyril Forbes' eye. He was not yet fully *'dehypnotised'*, the term his visitor used to describe his post-Wednesday condition. He was a slightly built man and had a peculiarly shaped head with the jutting chin and elaborately curved nose of a Punch in the best of seaside traditions. His eyes were deep set and dark and animated like those of an inquisitive parrot.

"I do wish you'd explain this irrational reverence you have for gravy," Mrs Charles said with a sigh.

"I thought I might be able to use it up some time or other," he defended himself.

She sighed again. "You've always been the same— even as a small child. I don't know, I'm sure. . . . It's just as well Mother and I, *one* of us, has always been around to keep an eye on you, otherwise the British Isles would now be surrounded by a veritable sea of stuff—no doubt with a quarter-inch growth on it!" She shuddered, rinsing out the offending mug under the hot-water tap.

She pointed to the other two mugs. "Is this all there is, Cyril? You haven't got some more of it tucked away somewhere—?"

"No," he said absently.

She went to the refrigerator and carefully examined its contents, then similarly checked the cupboards. Satisfied that all was as it should be, she returned to the sink and rinsed out the other mugs. Then she made ready to give all three a thorough wash in scalding hot water and strong detergent.

The rumbling sound of a heavy vehicle changing down into a lower gear as it turned off the access road from the motorway made her pause and raise her eyes to the window. She waited with her rubber-gloved knuckles resting lightly on the bottom of the washing-up bowl, and a little under a minute later a dark blue and yellow day-tour coach, the one hired by the Day Centre for its outing—Mrs Charles clearly recognised several of its elderly passengers—trundled heavily past and then temporarily vanished from view beyond an uninterrupted section of Cyril Forbes' undisciplined hawthorn hedge. Finally losing sight of it altogether, Mrs Charles glanced round at the wall clock: the coach was right on time for the cream tea at the vicarage.

"I want you to do a little job for me, Cyril," she said, thoughtfully drying one of the mugs on the clean cloth that she had taken from a drawer in the Welsh dresser.

"Yes, 'Del," he mumbled.

"I've put an advert. in the Personal columns of several daily newspapers. . . . The *Player*—Do you know what I'm talking about, Cyril?" She frowned at him. "The painting from Miss Player's sitting-room, the one I told you about . . . I must try and get it back." She paused and studied him thoughtfully. It was hard to tell, but she thought he was listening to her.

"Now," she continued, "on the offchance that the *Player's* present owner . . . goodness only knows how many times it's changed hands over the past five years, but if whoever now owns it replies to my advert., you will have to handle any resultant negotiations for me. I can't leave the village. Not with all the gossip that's going on about me. You know what people would think if I suddenly disappeared now." She paused, frowning. "Are you following me, Cyril?"

He gave a jerky nod of his head. "I'll have to be back by Wednesday—"

"Yes, of course," she said quickly. "This should only take a day, two at the most. I'm relying on you, Cyril. It is very important that you don't let me down."

"I understand." He nodded again, a preoccupied look still very much in evidence in his dark eyes. "Our fair-haired friend—he could still have it, you know."

The remark surprised Mrs Charles. She would not have expected anything like it from him for a while yet: he was obviously coming round much faster than she had suspected.

"*Friend?* I hardly think he would qualify for that distinction, Cyril." She gave him a very thoughtful look. "There are a lot of possibilities. The *Player* could even be out of the country . . . we'll just have to hope for the best."

"It's going to be like it used to be in the old days . . . the two of us working together."

"Not quite, Cyril." She spoke gently, as one would to a small child. "This could be dangerous, not at all like the old times. I want you to understand that quite clearly. I know how important the motorway is to you, but you're simply going to have to forget about it for a few days and concentrate on nothing but what I want you to do for me. And you must be careful, Cyril. *Very* careful. There's a very great deal at stake here. For both of us."

"I'll be careful, 'Del," he promised. "You know you can rely on me."

"Yes," she said slowly, eyeing him a little doubtfully. "Now I want you to listen carefully. Elaina Petrovic has agreed to handle any initial contact there might be: she will arrange a meeting and then this is where you will take over for me . . ."

"I won't have to go and see Elaina, will I?" he asked quickly, a sudden alarm bringing his gaze sharply into focus.

"No, Cyril," she smiled. "Not unless you particularly want to. . . ."

Margaret Sayer stood before the straight-sided decanter and eyed it critically. Cissie Keith was 'ooh-aahing' over it and swore it was early 19th-century Waterford, but Miss Sayer told her not to be such a silly cat and said that Cissie wouldn't know a piece of good cut-glass—Waterford or otherwise—if she fell over it!

The two women had slipped away from the rest of the coach-party on the pretext of finding some vaguely defined article of personal belonging which Mrs Keith claimed to have mislaid since leaving the coach and entering the vicarage (it was a well-known fact that Cissie Keith never went anywhere without losing something); but what she and Margaret Sayer were really doing was what they called 'having a quick look around'. They were, for the moment, in the Blackmores' private sitting-room. Everyone else was in the drawing-room, which was the largest reception-room in the vicarage and the one most suited for serving the cream tea which had been promised to the ladies and gentlemen of the Day Centre.

With a parting glare at the decanter, Margaret Sayer wandered over to the window and said, "She's always bent over backwards to try and make everyone believe that she's come from something a bit better than she really has."

"I don't think Mrs Blackmore's ever done anything of the sort," Cissie Keith swiftly defended their hostess. "She's not in the least bit snooty."

"No, and she wouldn't want to be!" Miss Sayer said, giving the other woman one of her heavily-hooded look. "I've heard a tale or two about that little madam. That friend who was staying with me last summer . . . the one who worked with me in London when I was with the Post Office . . . she used to be friendly with someone who knew Mrs Blackmore and her family quite well."

Cissie Keith eyed her suspiciously. "You've never mentioned anything about this before. . . ."

"What was the use? I wouldn't have got any thanks for knocking your little tin goddess off her pedestal, would I?"

"Then why bother to say anything now?" Cissie Keith retorted in a rare mood of defiance. It was not often that she stood up to Margaret Sayer, but when she did the exchange between them was usually quite heated. "Mrs Blackmore is a very nice lady and there isn't a soul in the village—aside from you, that is—who doesn't think so. Mr Blackmore is a very lucky man to have her for his wife: she's a great asset to him."

"If you'll just wait a minute and let me finish,"

Miss Sayer retaliated, full of indignation and ready for battle. "I wasn't talking so much about her as her family. Her father was a real villain. . . ."

Cissie Keith's defiant mood was still well to the fore. "Well," she snapped, "that's where you're wrong! He was an Anglican priest, like Mr Blackmore."

"So?" Miss Sayer said coldly. "What difference does that make? Villains come in all shapes and sizes and colours, and they can also wear all sorts of different disguises: but under the skin, my girl, they're all the same. Rotten to the core!"

Cissie Keith calmed down and became curious. "Do you mean that he, Mrs Blackmore's father, was an *imposter* . . . not really a man of the cloth at all?"

"Oh, no, that side of him was genuine enough . . . so far as it went. In fact, Gwen, my friend, said he was a real Tartar for putting the fear of God into everybody: his sermons were so full of fire and brimstone that most of his parishioners were terrified of him. Children actually screamed when they saw him coming, and Gwen said it got to be so bad . . . the way he was carrying on . . . that people started to complain and he finally had to be relieved of his duties. And do you know what the silly fool did? He decided that it was a sign from Heaven . . . that God was showing him the way to go . . . and so he took off his dog-collar and became one of these pavement prophets."

"Perhaps it *was* God's way of talking to him and he really did have a genuine calling for that type of preaching."

"You do say some daft things," Miss Sayer said irritably. "I honestly think you'd have a good word for the devil himself!"

"Well, I don't believe you should talk ill of somebody you don't really know anything about, like Mrs Blackmore's father. How do you know your friend wasn't just being spiteful?"

"Because I know people," Miss Sayer said darkly. "Just like I know that little madam. . . . . That fire and brimstone of her father's was just so much smoke, a screen to cover up his own evil desires."

"What evil desires?"

The vague look that suddenly appeared in Margaret Sayer's eye made Cissie Keith feel very cross with her. It was always the same. Margaret would hint at all manner of terrible things that people were supposed to have done, but it came to saying what those terrible things were, she didn't really know. . . .

Miss Sayer shrugged a little. "I don't know all the facts, but there was a woman involved . . . you can be sure of that!"

"Poor Mrs Blackmore," Cissie Keith said sympathetically. She gave Miss Sayer a very reproachful look. "It's not her fault that her father turned out to be bad."

"I never said it was!" Miss Sayer snapped. She swept a disdainful eye over the decidedly shabby room and made a face. "It must be donkey's years since any money has been spent on this room. I'm sure most of this furniture was here when I was a child. Some of it seems very familiar. I used to come here with my father and we often sat in this room . . . on that very same sofa there, going by the look of the state it's in. There's hardly anything covering the springs!"

"I think it's a very comfortable-looking room," the other woman said primly. "It's so like Mr Blackmore . . . solid and reliable. It gives me the feeling that it's all been here for ages and that it'll still be here, just as it is today, a hundred years from now. There's no feeling of permanence and continuity in new things. I'd hate to see this room altered in any way. I like it just as it is, worn-out sofa and all."

Margaret Sayer was tentatively fingering the dark green velour curtains. "Full of dust," she pronounced them. "The nets aren't much better. . . ." She had drawn them aside and was trying to guess when the window had last been cleaned.

Cissie Keith watched her in silence. Margaret had been very irritable and bad tempered these past few days, more so than usual. She went slowly back over the days in her mind, carefully adding them up. The final result confirmed her suspicion. Margaret was jealous . . . *jealous of her and Lionel*. She'd been peculiar ever since he'd arrived. . . .

They moved on to the Vicar's study.

"Isn't it romantic in here?" Cissie Keith said with a heart-felt '*aah*'.

Margaret Sayer shot her a withering look,.

"Think of it," Cissie Keith went on gushingly. "All the young couples over the years who must've come here to this room to talk to the Vicar about getting married. If wallpaper could only talk, what stories would be told. . . ."

Margaret Sayer stiffened and drew back into the doorway, but Cissie Keith didn't seem to notice that there was something amiss and moved further into the room, bestowing on it a smile that glowed with happy remembrances, some real, some imagined.

"I remember how it was when my Desmond and I went to see the Vicar of our church," she continued. "My Desmond felt we should've been quietly married at the Registry Office . . . because of our age . . . well, we weren't exactly in the first flush of youth, were we?—but I was determined to have a proper wedding . . . white gown and veil and all. I wouldn't have cared if I'd been ninety . . . I was walking down that aisle like a proper bride! Everybody said I'd make a fool of myself, but it was a beautiful wedding. They all said so afterwards. . . ."

She was suddenly aware that something was wrong and she looked round quickly. She was alone. Margaret Sayer had deserted her. Cissie Keith hurried out of the study and found her in the hall, but just as she was about to ask if there were anything the matter, Mrs Blackmore appeared in the drawing-room doorway.

"There you are, ladies," she smiled across at the two of them. "The cloakroom is at the other end of the hall . . . that door straight ahead of you."

"Oh, we didn't want to—"

Cissie Keith was silenced by a sharp elbow in her left side.

"We were just trying to find our way back to the others," Miss Sayer said quickly. "It's been so long since I was last inside the vicarage that I've forgotten my way about. I used to come here often, you know, with my father . . . when I was a small child. I'd quite forgotten how big it all is. I wonder that the Church has left it as it is and not turned it into a hostel of some kind or other . . . I mean, it's such a big place for just you and the Vicar on your own."

The three women walked into the drawing-room in companionable conversation, the general theme of which was big houses and the problems that went with them.

Mrs Keith's cousin and another man were sitting quietly together in a remote corner, where they appeared to be taking refuge from the members of the opposite sex who had them hopelessly outnumbered. The two men did not seem to be finding very much to say to one another and both looked relieved when they saw Mrs Keith and Miss Sayer making their way over to them.

The other man was John Billingsley, a retired army colonel. Colonel Billingsley had never been a handsome man, but he was one who nevertheless managed to stand out quite creditably in a crowd. The same could not have been said of his companion. Lionel Preston greeted his cousin with a glimmer of a smile, and then with a flickering glance at Miss Sayer, who had done her utmost all day to make him feel unwelcome and unwanted, he immediately withdrew into a crushed silence and nobody would have known that he was there.

The afternoon tea was laid out on what was probably the dining-room table and people mostly helped themselves from there, while the tea was poured and distributed round by the wives of the church-wardens who had volunteered their services for the afternoon.

Mrs Keith said everything was 'delicious', but Miss Sayer disagreed with her.

"This jam," she said, pulling a face round a mouthful of sticky scone. "It's got a funny taste. It's too sweet, sickly."

"It tastes all right to me," Cissie Keith said, looking with very wide eyes at the men. "It's very nice, isn't it?" she asked them, and they both nodded obediently.

"You'd say that about anything you didn't have to pay for out of your own pocket," Miss Sayer said harshly.

"The trouble today is that we're so conditioned to the rubbish that's foisted on us in the shops that we've forgotten what the real honest-to-goodness taste of homemade jam tastes like," Colonel Billingsley remarked.

"You're not going to tell me that Mrs Blackmore made this jam!" Miss Sayer exclaimed. "That's bought jam, if ever I tasted it! You just have to look at it . . . it's all pulp, no fruit."

"Strawberry jam is always like that," Cissie Keith said a little indistinctly. She finished what she was eating before attempting to continue. "It's always a lot sweeter than other jams, I always think."

"It's definitely home-made," Colonel Billingsley insisted. "Mrs Blackmore said so . . . while you were out of the room."

Miss Sayer got to her feet, put her plate to one side and went over to the table and peered into one of the almost empty jam dishes. Then she picked it up and sniffed its contents. "If that jam didn't come from Gidding's hypermarket," she said as she resumed her seat, "I'll eat my hat!"

"I should be careful what I said, if I were you, Margaret," Cissie Keith giggled. "Colonel Billingsley was just telling me that Mrs Charles made the jam. She brought it over to Mrs Blackmore yesterday specially for us."

Margaret Sayer glared at Colonel Billingsley. "I don't believe it," she said.

"Mrs Blackmore wouldn't say something like that if it wasn't true!" Cissie Keith maintained. "Why should she?"

Miss Sayer again put her plate aside and stalked off to find Mrs Blackmore. She was back in moments.

"Well?" Cissie Keith said. "What did she say? Mrs Charles did make the jam, didn't she?"

"That's what she told Mrs Blackmore," Miss Sayer replied thinly. "I still say it came off the shelf. . . ."

"Is everything all right here, ladies and gentlemen?" Mrs Blackmore smiled, coming up to them.

"Margaret . . . Miss Sayer thinks the jam—"

Cissie Keith scored another hefty nudge in the ribs and she took the hint and fell silent.

"The scones are very nice. . . . I wish I had your light touch," Miss Sayer said swiftly. "You did make them yourself?"

"Oh, yes," Mrs Blackmore said, and smiled again. "I'm glad you enjoyed them."

"You must give my niece, Jean, your secret," Miss Sayer said. "She uses far too much butter in her scones . . . I had indigestion for a whole day after I'd sampled the last lot she baked: she just doesn't seem to be able to get the mixture right. But some people never can, can they, no matter what they cook? It's always either too little of this or too much of that. . . ."

Mrs Blackmore made some appropriate comment about the vagaries of cooking and moved on to the next little group of people and had much the same sort of conversation with them.

"She doesn't look at all well, does she?" Cissie Keith commented when Mrs Blackmore was out of earshot. "She's very pale today."

"Mrs Charles' jam—it's much too sweet and sickly, and I've no doubt that we'll all suffer for it tomorrow," Margaret Sayer prognosticated.

CHAPTER EIGHT

At five minutes to midnight, Margaret Sayer was taken ill with what she thought was one of her bilious attacks. At exactly midnight, Anne Blackmore was carried out of the vicarage on a stretcher and put into a waiting ambulance.

Mr Blackmore had summoned their doctor shortly before eleven, after finding his wife lying semi-conscious on the kitchen floor. The doctor was reluctant to commit himself to a positive diagnosis and would go no further than to say that he suspected that Mrs Blackmore was suffering from some form of poisoning, food poisoning he seemed to think; and at his request, Mr Blackmore wrote down what, to the best of his knowledge, his wife had eaten and drunk during the preceding twenty-four hours. The doctor took this information over to the hospital in Gidding after advising Mr Blackmore what to do should he show symptoms of becoming similarly ill himself.

By the following morning, Mrs Blackmore was out of danger and resting comfortably. Miss Sayer was also feeling considerably better and although still a little weak after her unusually severe gastric upset of the previous night, managed to scribble a note to Miss Marsden advising her that she would not be attending the Day Centre for lunch that day as she was unwell. The neighbour who delivered the note for her returned with the news that the Day Centre was closed and that with about five exceptions, everyone who had gone on yesterday's outing was ill with what was widely thought to be salmonella food poisoning.

"They're saying in the village that Mrs Blackmore nearly died," Miss Sayer's neighbour added. "She was whisked off to hospital by ambulance in the middle of the night, and Mr Blackmore told Miss Marsden that the doctors over at the hospital in Gidding think it was something she ate yesterday lunch-time. Some inspectors from the Department of Health are going over to the hotel where you stopped for lunch yesterday to look at the kitchen and question the staff."

"They're wasting their time there: Mrs Blackmore didn't go on the outing," Miss Sayer snapped, her bite in no way affected by her present slight debility. "It must've been the cream tea we had at the vicarage yesterday afternoon. That's the only thing it could've been!"

"There'll be someone round to see you, too," the neighbour warned her. "It's just like it was when Miss Player was murdered," the woman added, her eyes bright with excitement. "They're questioning just about everybody ..."

A health inspector from the local authority interviewed Frank Blackmore that afternoon.

"I understand that your wife gave a cream tea here late yesterday afternoon," the inspector began his interrogation of the Vicar, getting out a notebook and a ballpoint pen.

"Yes," Mr Blackmore replied. "That is quite correct."

"I presume it was the traditional cream tea: scones—jam—cream?" the inspector wearily enumerated.

"Yes. My wife made the scones herself; one of the villagers provided the jam, and the cream came from Roper's Dairy, the one in the village—it was fresh that day."

The inspector nodded solemnly over the notes that he was making. He was an uncommonly tall man, every bit of six feet six inches, and was so thin that Frank Blackmore was moved to wonder if too much time spent tracking down harmful bacteria in food had destroyed the man's appetite to the point where he barely ate sufficient to keep himself alive.

"We had a word with Sam Roper and checked his dairy first thing this morning," the inspector said. "All clear there. The scones . . . I suppose your wife used packet flour?"

The Vicar nodded and took the inspector out to the kitchen and showed him the large, floor-standing earthenware jar from which Mrs Blackmore had taken the flour to make the scones.

The inspector peered into its depths. "Not very likely that we'll find anything wrong here, but you never know. . . ." He asked for a spoon and then took a sample of the flour which he sealed in a clear polythene bag. "What about the jam?" he enquired. "You said that was home-made?"

"Yes, but I'm afraid it was all used up," Mr Blackmore said apologetically. "I've never seen such healthy appetites. I always thought elderly people only picked at their food!"

The inspector was not listening. He was busy scrutinising the kitchen, his practised eye lighting on all the spots which the less hygiene conscious housewife overlooked. In due course he made a note in his little book to the effect that Mrs Blackmore kept her kitchen and its work-surfaces scrupulously clean.

"I can give you the empty jars . . . if that's any

good to you?" Mr Blackmore offered. "I have them out in the garage—I wasn't sure what to do with them . . . I thought my wife might want to return them to Mrs Charles, the lady who made the jam."

The inspector looked doubtful. "I don't think they'll tell us anything, not if they've been cleaned."

The Vicar smiled a little foolishly. "To be honest with you, I didn't bother about washing them . . . no sense in going to all that trouble if they were only going to be put in the dustbin. My wife wasn't feeling too well all afternoon, so I did some of the clearing up after the cream tea for her. I intended to ask her this morning what she wanted done with the jars."

At the inspector's request, the Vicar went out to the garage for the jam jars, each one of which was given a quick tentative sniff before being placed in another of the polythene bags which the inspector carried about with him.

"I understand you didn't eat anything yesterday afternoon?" the inspector said, the sudden arching of his eyebrows thinning his face and making it look considerably longer.

"No—I'm a diabetic and on a strict diet."

"Ah!" the inspector said, as if some great mystery had been solved.

"I must say I feel very embarrassed about this," the Vicar confessed, frowning. "My poor wife will be mortified when she hears what's happened."

"No need for that," the inspector assured him. "I doubt if we'll find our mystery bug anywhere here. The traces of jam left on the jars smelt perhaps a shade on the sugary-sweet side, but I think that'll be the only fault we'll find there. Still, one never knows," he added brightly. "Life is full of surprises, especially in our line of work. The most innocent-looking cooking utensil, for example, can harbour a horrific line up of deadly—"

He didn't finish. The Vicar had gone an odd colour.

"Very rare, of course," the inspector said, and hastily gathered up his samples and made his farewells.

CHAPTER NINE

The Reverend Frank Blackmore drove over to Gidding first thing on Monday morning to collect his wife from hospital. Mrs Blackmore was still a little pale, but she protested vigorously when it was suggested that she could be feeling anything but completely fit and well again, and complained that there had been a lot of fuss about nothing and generally seemed more concerned that her husband had either cooked for himself or been invited out to a hot mid-day meal following the previous day's morning service.

"How is the big investigation coming along?" she asked on the drive back to the village. "Have they traced the contaminated food yet?"

Her husband shook his head. "They don't seem to be any the wiser. I heard it will be some time before all the tests are completed."

"Has everyone recovered?"

"Mrs Hatchard hasn't quite got over it yet—but at her age that's hardly surprising. Mrs Keith had a bad time of it, too, though fortunately her cousin was one of those who wasn't affected and he was able to look after her."

Mrs Blackmore frowned concernedly. "I must call round there this afternoon and see her. And Mrs Hatchard. Then there's Mrs Charles—I don't suppose you had time to return her basket and the jam jars, so I'll drop them in to her while I'm out."

"I really think you should give yourself a little more time to recover your strength before you start dashing about and seeing everybody. No one would expect it of you. That was a very sick lady they took away in the middle of last Thursday night, my dear," he reminded her soberly. "I phoned Mrs Charles over the weekend and thanked her for the jam and she said there was no hurry about the basket: I'm quite sure she can manage another day or two without it; and there aren't any jars to return to her. The health inspector took them away with him."

She gave him a startled look. "They think there was something wrong with Mrs Charles' jam?"

"No, I don't think so. The inspector said it smelt a little sweet to him, but that was the only comment he made about it."

"It tasted all right to me," she said.

"Yes—but we all know about that hollow sweet tooth of yours, don't we?" He smiled at her affectionately.

They turned off the access road from the motorway on to a roundabout which they then left by the first exit. Seconds later, a white-helmeted motor-cyclist shot round a bend a hundred yards or so ahead of them. Mrs Blackmore's head followed his progress, her eyes fastened on his leather-jacketed back.

"That was Cyril Forbes, wasn't it?" she remarked. "He's going somewhere in an awful hurry." She frowned. "I thought he always walked over to the motorway. And today is Monday, not Wednesday. He must be going over to Gidding." She looked at her husband and widened her eyes. "I wonder what he wants over there?"

"If I'd realised you were so interested to know what

he's up to, I would've flashed the headlamps at him to stop and you could've asked him," he said dryly.

"I was trying to be serious," Jean Sayer said with a fierce glare at her protagonist. "It isn't a bit funny. Your aunt seriously believes that Mrs Charles has tried to poison her and the others."

"*What?* All forty-eight of them?" Her husband smiled. "Why? What dreadful secret do the members of the Day Centre know about Mrs Charles that the rest of the village has yet to hear?"

"Not *them*: Cissie Keith and her cousin! Your aunt maintains that they know something else about Mrs Charles, something she doesn't want spread round the village; and Auntie says that the only way she can prevent that from happening is to get rid of them before they can talk."

It was difficult, but David Sayer managed to keep a straight face. "Was she successful?" he enquired.

"Who—Mrs Charles? Of course not! Auntie said that Lionel Preston was one of those who wasn't ill after the outing. But Cissie Keith was dreadfully sick."

"Sloppy of Mrs Charles to get one and not the other," he remarked, still very straight-faced. "I wonder how she managed that?"

"You don't think there could be something in what your aunt says?"

He shook his head.

"Why not?" his wife persisted.

He gazed at her for a very long moment. "You know you're getting as silly as the old girl, don't you? Sillier, in fact."

She glared at him, then her expression relaxed and she grinned a little. "Silly or not, your aunt says there's a big investigation under way in the village.

She's expecting to be interviewed by an inspector from the Department of Health some time this afternoon."

"If all the excitement doesn't finish her off in the meantime," he said dryly. "I must say the poor chap has my sympathy. I should imagine that half an hour with my Aunt Margaret and her half-baked ideas on a mass poisoner of a lot of dear old chatterboxes and he'll be praying for a nice quiet outbreak of typhoid—preferably a couple of hundred miles away!"

Jean Sayer smiled. Her pale grey eyes studied him thoughtfully. He had been unusually quiet these past four or five days, ever since going over to the village to see Mrs Charles . . . very much absorbed in his thoughts.

"You can't make up your mind about Mrs Charles, can you?" she remarked at length.

"No," he admitted, his tone a trifle short.

"What did Fred Church have to say about her?"

He shot her a quick, surprised look.

"How did you know that I've been talking to him?"

"I didn't. I'm not just a pretty face, you know: I haven't lived with a police officer all these years and not learned a trick or two of my own . . . like how to put two and two together! You said Fred was in charge of the Stuart murder investigation, so I guessed you'd get around to him sooner or later. And," she went on with a small smile, "you have rather lost touch with one another since he was transferred up north. No time like the present for renewing old acquaintanceships . . . isn't that right?"

She widened her eyes a little at the ensuing tight-lipped silence. "Well, go on!" she exclaimed. "Don't keep me in suspense . . . cross my heart and hope to die if I ever breathe a word. My lips are sealed! Now tell me what he said about Mrs Charles."

"Adele Herrmann," he corrected her, and smiled. "She didn't marry Edwin Charles until after the Stuart murder. Fred only knew her by her maiden name, though he did say he was aware that there had been the odd husband or two flitting about in her past."

"Did she murder Janet Stuart?"

He shrugged his shoulders. "Fred thinks so. The evidence against her was too circumstantial: they had to let her go and hope she'd make a slip. She made her way down to London and set up shop there. Same sort of business—reading palms, the Tarot, gazing into the crystal ball. . . . They kept an eye on her for the next year or so, but she kept strictly to the letter of the law. Then she disappeared again and that was it: they could find no trace of her anywhere. Obviously that was when she teamed up with Edwin Charles. She told me he was a circus performer—" He paused and frowned. "At least, I assume that he was the circus performer . . . so they were probably on the move a fair bit, touring round the countryside. Until she got tired of the life, or of him, or of both, and decided to retire to the village and start a new life."

"With the Punch and Judy man?" she asked, her eyebrows raised expectantly.

"With her brother," he said flatly. "Cyril Forbes is Adele Herrmann's half-brother. Same mother, different fathers. The mother appears to have gone through as many husbands as the daughter has!"

"Did Mrs Charles tell you that?"

"No, Fred did."

David Sayer frowned and shook his head. "She's a close one. Clever. Too clever to have a go at poisoning off a goodly slice of the village elderly because she wants to still the one or two nasty little wagging tongues in their midst. I'm certain she knows a good deal more about the Stuart murder than she has let on to me . . . and to Fred and his lot. But that doesn't necessarily make her the guilty party."

"She could be protecting someone."

"Cyril Forbes?" He looked doubtful. "I can't see it myself. Forbes is too soft in the head for that sort of brutal crime."

"But the Stuart murder was committed ten years ago. Who's to say what Cyril Forbes was like then? And look how het up he got over the motorway! He hit a councillor over the head with the placard he was carrying that time, don't forget!"

David Sayer said he remembered. He also said that there were a good many people, including himself, who had often wished that they had had the courage to deal similarly with that particular local politician. "Which does not make any one of us, or the brave soul who actually performed the deed, either a murderer or capable of murder," he finished.

"I suppose not," she agreed hesitantly. "Did you mention Henrietta Player to Fred?"

"Only briefly. He was sharp enough to realise that there was a very good reason for my sudden interest in the Stuart murder and Adele Herrmann, so I couldn't really avoid mentioning anything about Henrietta Player. He seemed to think I could be on to something and wanted me to make it official; but even if I did talk things over with the Gidding lads, I can't see that they would get any further now than we got five and a half years ago when we made our original enquiries. If Mrs Charles did murder Henrietta Player, then she will have covered up her tracks as expertly as she did ten years ago when—*if*—she committed the Stuart murder. A series of coincidences, that's all I've really got against the woman, and that's not good enough. It's all too circumstantial. I need more," he went on quietly, almost to himself. "Something I can really get my teeth into . . . then I'll take the matter further and see it becomes official. But not before. . . ."

CHAPTER TEN

"I've never met the woman," Mary Sutherland, a small bird-like woman, confessed. "And really, from the gossip one has been hearing about her, I'm not at all sure that I would want to. She sounds a thoroughly bad lot: as wicked and evil as they come!"

"You'll have to make allowances for Mary." James Sutherland grinned at Jean Sayer from the doorway. He was followed into the kitchen, where his wife was preparing a salad for lunch, by David Sayer who had gone off with him a short while earlier to see how the builders were progressing with their work on the veterinary surgery which James Sutherland was planning to open up in Gidding in partnership with another veterinarian sometime early in the spring. David Sayer was supervising the security installations for the new premises.

Still grinning, James Sutherland continued:

"She's started watching the late night horror movie on televison again, and it's quite incredible what it does to her imagination. . . . Mrs Charles wouldn't hurt a fly! She's a very nice, good-natured, intelligent woman whose only sin, as far as I can see, is that of refusing to conform to the norm."

"You talk as though you know her pretty well," David Sayer observed.

"Well, you know how it is—people and their pets!"

James Sutherland raised his dark, shaggy eyebrows expressively. "As with one's family doctor, a fairly intimate relationship quite often develops over the years between a veterinarian and the owner of the pet he's always tended."

"I don't know that I like the sound of that," Mary Sutherland laughed.

"I think you know what I mean, dear," her husband smiled. "People say things to their doctor—and to a veterinarian—that they wouldn't dream of saying to anyone else, sometimes not even to members of their own families. There's always the exception, of course, but generally speaking, sickness lowers all barriers of inhibition. As was the case with Mrs Charles. It's a good few years ago now . . . four, maybe five . . . but she called me out once to look at that Capuchin of hers. Too late, I'm afraid. The poor little thing died a few seconds before I got there. Poisoned. Mrs Charles was dreadfully upset about it: she—"

James Sutherland broke off. The Sutherlands and the Sayers had been close friends for years, and James Sutherland would have said that he understood both David and Jean fairly well, well enough to know when they were deeply disturbed about something, but he couldn't think what he had said or done to cause them to feel that way.

"Did I say something wrong?" he asked, frowning.

"Poisoned?" David Sayer repeated in a strange voice. "That monkey Mrs Charles used to have was *poisoned*?"

"Yes, that's right. Why?"

"What sort of poison was it?"

"I don't know. . . . The symptoms that Mrs Charles related to me were consistent with those produced by at least three that came immediately to mind. I suggested an autopsy, but Mrs Charles wouldn't hear of it."

"But you must have had some idea?" David Sayer said, a trifle sharply.

James Sutherland glanced at Jean, noticed how pale she had become, and then looked back at David and laughed a little. "Look, what is this? The Spanish Inquisition all over again?"

Jean Sayer replied. "David's Aunt Margaret rang me just before we left to come over here this morning . . . she thinks Mrs Charles tried to poison Cissie Keith and Lionel Preston, Cissie's cousin . . . he's staying with her at the moment. He's the one who started all this talk about Mrs Charles and that other unsolved murder," she explained when all she drew from the Sutherlands was a very blank look.

"Oh, yes, I remember," James Sutherland said thoughtfully, and his wife nodded. "No wonder you both went a bit green under the gills. You said 'tried', Jean: does that mean something went horribly wrong with Mrs Charles' plans for Cissie and cousin?"

"Yes and no . . . I mean, if the jam really was poisoned—" she blurted out, the words tumbling one over the other.

James Sutherland held up a hand. "Now, what say you calm down and go right back to the beginning and tell your nice Uncle Jim all about it? This gets more confusing by the minute," he grinned in an aside to his wife. Then, coming back to Jean: "What jam?"

David Sayer stepped in and briefly acquainted the Sutherlands with his Aunt Margaret's suspicions about the home-made strawberry jam which she and her friends from the Day Centre had eaten only a matter of hours, in some instances, before most of them became ill. As he finished, James Sutherland grinned at him and said:

"So what you'd now like me to tell you is that Mrs Charles' Capuchin partook of a nice cup of tea and a poisoned strawberry jam sandwich shortly before she—it was a female—passed on?"

"I suppose it is a bit far-fetched," Jean Sayer conceded, taking her cue from his tone of voice.

"No, not really," he surprised her by saying. "Stranger things have happened." He paused deliberately: then with a sly grin, he added: "But I don't think anything like that occurred in this instance.

"Mrs Charles was working in her garden," the veterinarian went on. "The Capuchin was out there with her and, as far as Mrs Charles was concerned, there was absolutely nothing wrong with her: the monkey was its perfectly normal mischievous self . . . kept nipping up behind her while she was digging and whizzing off with this and that—made a general nuisance of itself, as was its custom. Then after a while they both went inside, and seconds later the Capuchin went berserk . . . tearing out its fur and flying about the house screaming as if it were possessed. Mrs Charles eventually managed to get hold of it and she noticed that a patch of skin on its stomach, which was fairly devoid of fur, was covered in large angry-looking bumps . . . hives—like those one sees with an allergy—so she immediately contacted me.

"But, as I said, by the time I got to her it was too late. The poison had done its job. Directly or indirectly . . . the Capuchin was getting on a bit and I was inclined to think that she'd suffered a heart attack. A younger animal with a stronger constitution might've pulled through . . . been violently sick and had a bad tummy-ache for a time but otherwise suffered no lasting ill-effects from its gastronomic adventure. To begin with, I suspected that the Capuchin had got hold of some chemical fertiliser on a pesticide and had had itself a jolly good meal of one or the other while Mrs Charles was occupied with her digging, but she said that that was right out of the question. She told me that she was always most particular about weed-killers and the like and said that nothing dangerous was ever left where the Capuchin could get at it. And she was most emphatic that she hadn't been using anything of that nature that day. She said she was merely preparing a bed for some flowers: turning over the soil and weeding it by hand."

"So what did the monkey get hold of and eat?" It was Jean Sayer who asked the question.

"Well—" James Sutherland paused and shrugged a little. "Its paws were covered in soil," he thoughtfully recalled. "My belief is that while Mrs Charles was busy digging away at her little plot of ground, the Capuchin was doing likewise elsewhere. There's a lot of virgin soil around Mrs Charles' bungalow, a lot of wild plants . . . some very dangerous ones, especially in that wood at the bottom of her garden. I think the monkey dug up a root or a plant of some kind: it looked tasty and so she ate it—which theory is consistent with some vomit that Mrs Charles showed me. There was a great deal of soil present, bits of grass and what could've been a piece of root from some wild plant or other."

"Did Mrs Charles show any trace of alarm when you suggested an autopsy to determine the cause of death?" David Sayer asked.

"No. Only the distress that some owners display when a loved pet has died and such a thing has been suggested to them. There aren't many who like the idea of it. Of course, speaking strictly for myself, if it had been left to me to dispose of the remains—"

David Sayer didn't let his friend finish. "Mrs Charles buried the monkey herself? Somewhere in her garden?"

"I presume so: I didn't ask what her intentions were in that direction, but it's what people usually do when a pet dies. A lot of pets get a better send-off down the bottom of the garden than their owners would ever be likely to consider giving their nearest and dearest." James Sutherland grinned at his friends. "Come on, you two: you're taking dear old Aunt Maggots far too seriously. I can't see Edwina Charles poisoning anybody, intentionally or otherwise. And that's what you're both thinking, isn't it? That Mrs Charles keeps deadly poison of one kind or another about the place and that she wasn't telling me the truth about what happened to her monkey that day?" His grin widened and he wagged his head at them. "Oh, dear me . . . home-made strawberry jam indeed! Poor Mrs Charles!"

"You said it yourself," David Sayer said abruptly. "Stranger things have happened. But . . ." He paused and then shook his head. "No!" he enunciated firmly and fell silent.

Mary Sutherland laughed and said, "Well, go on: you can't leave things up in the air like that, David. No *what*?"

Jean Sayer smiled. "Mrs Charles has had a tremendous impact on David: he's not been the same person since he went over to the village the other day to see her. Just as well I'm not the jealous type, otherwise I should probably be turning quite nasty about his infatuation with her."

David Sayer gave a little laugh. "*Fear*, Jean: you've

completely misinterpreted the signs. The truth of the matter is that Mrs Charles scares me silly."

"You think she murdered that woman like they're saying in the village?" Mary Sutherland asked him, wide-eyed.

"Between ourselves . . . yes," he replied. "And yet—" He rubbed his right hand back and forth across his chin and looked troubled. "It's an odd thing, but every time I sort out my thinking and come up with a definite *yes* to that question—one I must've asked myself a hundred times over these past few days—I always find myself wanting to qualify . . . *limit* that 'yes' by adding that she was capable of it, committing murder . . . as if—as if lurking in the back of my mind there's some definite doubt about it. So what, I ask myself, am I doubtful about? And the answer has to be that I can't quite visualise Mrs Charles carrying out the crime itself, the actual physical part of it. *Plan it,* yes. . . ."

"You mean she was the *Mrs Big* who put someone else up to it?" Mary Sutherland wanted to know.

"Yes," David Sayer replied. "That I could accept. If Mrs. Charles is a criminal, then in my opinion she would certainly come into the big operator class and wouldn't be your common or garden variety villain, the underling who carries out the crime . . . does the dirty work. I sincerely believe that if Mrs Charles had wanted to get rid of Lionel Preston and Cissie Keith, we wouldn't be standing around here this morning wasting our time speculating about dead monkeys and strawberry jam and the rest of it. Lionel Preston and Cissie Keith would've been gonners, no mistake about it."

"Maybe she lost her cool?" Mary Sutherland put forward. "Cissie Keith's cousin might've got her rattled."

"*Never,*" David Sayer said with feeling. "She hasn't got away with murder for ten years—lived with it all that time—to be panicked now into doing something rash because a rather feeble-minded relic from her past has chanced to wander into the village and started telling tales about her. Mrs Charles puts me in mind of a spider—" He paused and thought for a moment. "Yes," he went on slowly. "That's exactly how I see Mrs Charles. She's a spider high on the wall, sitting up there in her web, sleek and self-assured, watching us all, taking everything in. She knows she's safe: she just has to keep perfectly still and wait for all the nasty troublesome predators to go away. . . ."

CHAPTER ELEVEN

Cissie Keith smiled wanly beneath her frayed orange hair as Lionel Preston fussed about her, plumping up cushions and stuffing them behind her back. She was enjoying every minute of the attention that she was getting which her visitor, Anne Blackmore, was sure would delay her 'recovery' quite considerably. Lionel Preston was obviously very fond of her and she of him, though perhaps not quite so apparently, Anne Blackmore thought, and for the moment they were so completely wrapped up in one another that they were aware of no one but themselves.

She watched them with a mixture of curiosity and pity. Cissie and her late husband, Desmond, had moved from London to the village eight years ago—at about the time, Anne Blackmore recalled, that she and Frank had just more or less finished settling into the vicarage. Then, six months later, Desmond Keith died, leaving Cissie alone after what had been a brief but by all accounts ecstatically happy five years together. It had been a first and very late marriage for both of them and although Cissie lived frugally and freely admitted herself that most of her clothes were bought second-hand, Anne Blackmore had heard it rumoured that she had been left very well provided for. She had never given the impression that she was lonely and seemed to get along well enough with her own age group, but she was one of those insipid, mindless women, Anne Blackmore decided as she patiently waited for Cissie to finish directing Lionel Preston's ministrations, who blossom maddeningly when they have a man about them. Anne Blackmore had had a friend just like it, and she never thought about her without experiencing some very mixed feelings of frustration and extreme irritability. Cissie Keith was beginning to have much the same effect on her.

Lionel was a bachelor and a first cousin on his mother's side, Cissie had whispered to her when he had absented himself from the room for a few moments while he went to fetch the rug that he was now busily tucking round Cissie's ankles. Anne Blackmore vaguely recalled having been introduced to him at the vicarage last Thursday afternoon, but she couldn't for the moment remember what had become of him after that initial meeting. She studied him thoughtfully, and a muzzy picture began to form itself in her mind of a pale, introverted, myopic little man sitting with and yet somehow apart from Mrs Keith, Miss Sayer and Colonel Billingsley—a quite different man, Anne Blackmore smiled to herself, from the one that she was seeing today.

With Cissie settled comfortably on the sofa and the gas fire burning brightly and the curtain over the door to the hall drawn to keep out any stray draught (Anne Blackmore thought she would scream if Lionel Preston didn't soon stop fussing), Lionel felt he could safely withdraw to the kitchen, where he then bustled about getting the afternoon tea. Left on their own, the two women immediately plunged into an intimate exchange of case histories, one hardly listening to the other, which they kept up until the afternoon tea-tray was brought in. The subject was then changed and became less personal.

"Lionel and I were talking about Madame Adele—I mean Mrs Charles—just before you came . . . I find it so hard to call Mrs Charles *Mrs Charles* now that I know her real name," Cissie Keith simpered. "Margaret—Miss Sayer—said there was something wrong with the jam that Mrs Charles gave you for the cream tea we had at the vicarage last Thursday . . ."

Mrs Blackmore gave her a startled look. "What do you mean?"

"Miss Sayer thinks it was poisoned, but she doesn't expect that anyone will ever be able to prove it. She said there are some poisons which can't be detected."

Another time, the solemn, purse-lipped expression on Cissie Keith's face would have appeared comical to Anne Blackmore, but in this instance, the nonsense behind it had dulled her sense of the ridiculous. What was being suggested was no laughing matter.

"That's a dreadful thing to say," she rebuked her with a little frown. "You should know better than to take any notice of what Margaret Sayer tells you: there are times when she lets her imagination run completely away with her."

"She does get a bit carried away with herself," Cissie Keith admitted with a small sigh. "I sometimes wonder if it's because she hasn't had much excitement in her life; but then that can't be true. She held down a very responsible supervisory job high up in the Civil Service right up until the time she retired."

"Oh—I thought she'd always lived in the village?" Mrs Blackmore said interrogatively. "Didn't she stay at home and look after her parents?"

"No, not until after she retired. She left the Civil Service when she was sixty, and her mother and father were well into their eighties by then. She returned home to look after them about nine years ago, not much more than a year before my late husband and I moved here; and as you know, the old people died three years later, within weeks of one another. She left the village, or so I was told, when she was in her twenties . . . after an unfortunate love affair with an absolute scoundrel who already had a wife."

Mrs Blackmore was nodding her head. "Yes, I heard all about it. Miss Sayer married him. . . ."

"Yes: the wedding service was actually held in St Stephen's and most of the village, I believe, turned out for it—I daresay you know that Miss Sayer's father used to be the village doctor . . . the whole Sayer family was very well liked by everyone, highly respected. Then Dr Sayer, Margaret's father, found out that the man was already married, a bigamist! Margaret never forgave her father for it and she left home. They only patched up their differences when she heard that the old people were ill and she came home to see them."

Mrs Blackmore frowned a little. "I feel very sorry for Miss Sayer: no one could say that she's had a happy life; but I don't think there is any excuse for her present vindictiveness towards Mrs Charles."

Mrs Blackmore transferred her gaze to Lionel Preston and was puzzled by the strange way in which he was regarding her. He made no attempt to disagree with the remarks that she had just made, but she couldn't help feeling that they, or something else that had just been said, had upset him in some way.

Cissie Keith studied her visitor curiously. "We were all terribly surprised about the jam," she said after a moment. "I mean, nobody realised that you and the Vicar were so friendly with Mrs Charles. None of us can ever remember seeing her in church . . . though Margaret says that that's probably because

Mrs Charles has been divorced so many times. The Church doesn't really like divorce, does it? And Lionel says that Mrs Charles has had more husbands than he's had hot dinners!"

"Adele Herrmann wouldn't have the nerve to step inside the House of God," Lionel Preston said in a high-pitched, giggly voice. "It would be sacrilege: she's evil, a witch!"

"Really, Mr Preston!" Mrs Blackmore exclaimed. "I don't think you should—"

"You don't know her like I do, Mrs Blackmore," he solemnly interrupted. "You haven't seen her wickedness first-hand like I have."

"You certainly seem to be most familiar with her past activities," Mrs Blackmore said curtly. "If I may be so impertinent as to ask, Mr Preston: just how do you know so much about Mrs Charles?"

"I was the one who tried to get the necklace back!" Behind his thick-lensed spectacles, Lionel Preston's brown eyes were large and moist and held an innocence that clashed discordantly with the thin, smug little smile on his lips.

"What necklace?" Puzzled, Mrs Blackmore looked to Mrs Keith for an answer.

"You don't know about that?" Cissie Keith looked quite astonished. "Mrs Charles stole a necklace from that poor woman she murdered ten years ago . . . Mrs Stuart. Lionel was a clerk with the firm of solicitors who acted for Mrs Stuart, and after she was murdered they sent him round to Madame . . . I mean Mrs Charles' home to ask her to hand it over— Which," she went on, hardly pausing for breath and with splotches of excited colour rising on her neck, "any other person would've done under the circumstances . . . you know, if they'd come by the necklace the way she said she had. I mean to say, you just have to ask yourself, don't you? If it was true and Mrs Stuart did give her the necklace, then all I can say is that it would've been obvious to any decent, honest person that the poor woman was well, a bit funny in the head. No one in their right mind gives a valuable diamond necklace away to a complete stranger. And that's what Mrs Charles expected everyone to believe."

Mrs Blackmore looked shocked and bewildered. "What did Mrs Charles say when you went to see her about giving the necklace back?" she asked Lionel Preston.

"She just stood and laughed at me and told me to tell my employers what they could do! You can take my word for it, Mrs Blackmore: Adele Herrmann is not a very nice person!"

"Good heavens," Mrs Blackmore murmured. "I simply don't know what to think!"

"Tell Mrs Blackmore about the will, Lionel." Cissie Keith's prominent front teeth shone yellow in the pale glow from the table-lamp which had been switched on as the shadows of the late winter afternoon had lengthened.

"Oh, yes," he said slowly, then gazed reflectively out of the window at the leaden skies. "That must've been about a month before Mrs Stuart was murdered. We . . . that is myself and one of the principals of the firm which employed me," he continued, looking round at Mrs Blackmore, "went out to Mrs Stuart's home to get her signature on her will. I'll never forget that day," he fervently assured his cousin. "Never as long as I live! Mrs Stuart was terrified, positively terrified . . . kept changing her mind . . . it was really most extraordinary: one minute she was going to sign, the next she was refusing to have anything to do with us."

Coming back to Mrs Blackmore, he then went on:

"My employer didn't know what to make of her attitude, though it seemed pretty obvious to me, especially in the light of some of her recent behaviour . . . there had been a costly interlude with some religious cranks—if you'll pardon me for calling them that, Mrs Blackmore—immediately preceding her involvement with Adele Herrmann . . . that she was becoming senile. Senile dementia is not at all uncommon in people of Mrs Stuart's years," he gravely intoned, pausing momentarily for effect and then continuing—

"Mrs Stuart kept insisting that she would die if she signed the will—admittedly, a sentiment a great many perfectly sane people entertain about the making of a will—but in Mrs Stuart's case, her attitude was quite extreme, quite irrational; and finally, my employer said we would go and suggested that she should come in to the office and see him when she felt that she was ready to sign the document. She became even more frightened then and begged us not to leave. . . ."

"Did she ever sign the will?" Mrs Blackmore probed.

Lionel Preston was gazing out of the window again. There was something odd about the expression on his face: he looked vaguely disturbed and frowned when Mrs Blackmore spoke, as if he resented the intrusion on his thoughts. It was a moment or two before he responded.

"Yes, eventually," he sighed. "But dear me, what a performance we had: I'll never forget it!"

"Was there something in the will that she didn't like?" Mrs Blackmore queried with a puzzled frown.

"No, no—" he quickly assured her, returning her frown. "You've missed the point completely, Mrs Blackmore. The will was perfectly straightforward and drawn up strictly in accordance with Mrs Stuart's instructions. A sister-in-law who lived in America was her sole beneficiary. No . . . in refusing at first to sign the will, Mrs Stuart was undoubtedly acting under the influence of Adele Herrmann who had been bleeding her white for goodness knows how long. The necklace that Adele Herrmann stole from her was just the tip of the iceberg, so to speak. I can tell you—in strict confidence, of course—that Mrs Stuart had been an exceedingly wealthy woman, but she went to her grave practically penniless, a pauper!"

"Oh dear," Mrs Blackmore murmured, widening her eyes at Cissie Keith, who nodded her endorsement of all that her cousin had said. "I can't understand how Mrs Charles got away with it," Mrs Blackmore remarked after a short pause.

"No one could," Lionel Preston said with an effeminate little shrug. "Especially as the police were so sure that Mrs Stuart had been murdered by a woman." He wrinkled his nose girlishly. "It was a particularly gruesome, messy murder. My employer saw the official police photographs of the poor woman's body and he was quite ill for days afterwards. He told me that the police surgeon said that two or three blows at the very most should've been all that a man of average strength would have needed to inflict on poor Mrs Stuart's head to bring about her death, whereas, in actual fact, it had taken many, many more blows than that to kill her. This, I believe, is what primarily led the police to conclude that she'd been murdered by a woman . . . someone of similar weight and strength to her own, which was far from robust. I understand that there was no evidence of any struggle at the scene of the crime, but nevertheless, Mrs Stuart did not give up her life easily. In spirit if not physically, she fought to the death, as they say," he finished soberly.

"How awful," Mrs Blackmore said with feeling. "It seems monstrous to me that someone could get away with such a brutal, callous crime."

"And twice at that," Lionel Preston said. "Cissie has been telling me about that woman here in the village . . . Henrietta Player; and you'll never convince me that poor soul wasn't Adele Herrmann's next victim."

Cissie Keith shuddered. "Stop it, Lionel!" she said quickly. "You're frightening me. You and Margaret Sayer are a good pair! For goodness' sake talk about something else. . . ."

CHAPTER TWELVE

Lionel Preston walked with Anne Blackmore to her car which she had left parked in the High Street, just around the corner from his cousin's tiny end-of-terrace cottage. There they parted and went their separate ways, Mrs Blackmore to see elderly Mrs Hatchard, who had not completely recovered from the gastric upset which she, in common with forty-two of the forty-eight members of the Day Centre who had gone on last Thursday's outing, had suffered (if there were time, Mrs Blackmore also hoped to return Mrs Charles' shopping-basket to her); while Lionel Preston, who had expressed a desire for some fresh air after a weekend spent indoors ministering to his sick cousin, was going to walk over to the motorway—weather permitting. His cousin and Mrs Blackmore had both tried to persuade him to delay his walk until the following day when better weather was promised for the district, but he had decided to chance that it would not rain before his return.

It had started to drizzle long before Mrs Blackmore lost sight of him, but he didn't turn back as she expected. He simply lowered his head and kept resolutely on—as if, Mrs Blackmore mused, he had a very definite purpose in mind and not just some hazy inclination to walk as far as the motorway and back. A sudden thought struck her as she started up her car and she wondered if what she were thinking could possibly be true. *But why?* she asked herself, frowning. *Why would Lionel Preston want to go calling on Edwina Charles?*

Lionel Preston kept his head down and looked neither to the right nor to the left, mainly because the fine rain misted over the lenses in his spectacles that much quicker if he held his head erect. He could see very little without the aid of spectacles and, in this kind of weather, not much more with them on. He had to keep pausing to wipe them over with his handkerchief and very much regretted that he had not taken the precaution of bringing an umbrella out with him.

He felt Margaret Sayer's eyes on him as he hurried towards her neat detached cottage. She was sitting at her living-room window with a cup of tea in her hand, and her eyes narrowed speculatively as she watched him go by. *Where on earth did the fool think he was going in this weather?* she asked herself, leaning forward to keep him in her sights for as long as possible. And on his own! That cat Cissie hardly ever let him out of her sight . . . probably afraid that someone would snatch him from under her nose and run off with him!

Miss Sayer sat back in her chair for a moment while she deliberated over his probable destination. He was heading in the direction of the motorway: but what did he want with the motorway? Motorways were for people in cars, she reasoned. No, Lionel Preston was on his way to see *that woman,* and Miss Sayer couldn't say that she was in the least bit surprised. It was, in her opinion, a natural sequence of events. Craning her neck forward, she watched him until he disappeared from sight. Yes, she frowned, he was definitely on his way over to see Edwina Charles.

Miss Sayer looked at the time: it was a little after three thirty.

Lionel Preston lingered for quite some time in the wood which ran along the bottom of Mrs Charles' garden, sheltering from the rain on the perimeter of a small clearing where a rusted axe leaned forgotten against a jumble of wet, mossy logs. Somewhere around four fifteen, he left the wood and set off across open fields towards the now derelict White-thatch Cottage which had once been the home of Henrietta Player and her artist father. Lionel Preston barely gave it a glance as he hurried by.

Cyril Forbes' property was a quarter of a mile further on, the last house before one came to the motor-way, and Lionel Preston made straight for it. He hoped that he would find Cyril Forbes at home, but was disappointed. No one answered his knock and the whole place had such a desolate, deserted air about it that he was sure that Cyril Forbes was nowhere about and hadn't been for some time.

He waited around for a while and then, when the rain got heavier, he reluctantly decided to return to the village. He set off back the way he had come, frowning absently over the conversation that his cousin had had a short while earlier with Ann Blackmore about Margaret Sayer. . . . . Who *had* come to the village first? he worried to himself. The other day, Cissie said that the Punch and Judy man came there at the beginning of 'sixty-six. Surely that was a mistake? And how relevant was it who was here first? he asked himself uneasily. He shivered a little, and not entirely with the cold. If Cyril Forbes confirmed that he was the first to arrive in the village, what then? Day after day, haunted by the memory of the sick, frightened look on another man's face

. . . was that how it was going to be from now on? he wondered miserably. Office gossip, rumours of insanity, more than half-forgotten over the years, suddenly crowded his thoughts. *Why had he been sworn to secrecy on just that one point?* The reasons given had seemed valid enough at the time; but now he wondered . . . wondered about a lot of things, he thought bitterly. He cursed himself out loud for his stupidity. The two of them, they'd been in it together and he hadn't seen it. . . . Cissie was always telling him how naïve he was, especially about women.

He sheltered again in the wood beyond Mrs Charles' large back garden. There was no light showing in any of the rear diamond-pane windows of her bungalow as there had been when he had passed that way an hour or so earlier.

He was polishing his spectacles when he heard the noise. A fox, he thought at first. He quickly put on the smeary spectacles and looked nervously round in the direction of the sound, but their lenses became splattered with raindrops from the overhanging branch of a tree and he was obliged to remove them almost immediately and polish them dry again. Then he heard another noise which definitely had nothing to do with a fox or any other four-legged creature. It was a repetitive sound, like that of a stick or some similar object being beaten against a tree trunk. There was a hypnotic quality to it and he felt himself drawn deeper into the wood to investigate. The nearer he came to the sound the surer he was of its origins. Someone was in the clearing chopping wood.

Anne Blackmore waited on Mrs Charles' front porch, clutching the latter's *Little Red Riding Hood* basket to her like a child seeking comfort and reassurance from some treasured possession. It was cold and raining and getting dark, and while Mrs Blackmore waited for Mrs Charles to answer the door, she wondered how foolish she had been in coming alone to this isolated place so late in the day. Perversely, instead of alarming her, the thought shocked some sense into her and she told herself that she was behaving as idiotically as the flock of sheep which had milled senselessly around her car some minutes earlier, mindless of the efforts of their shepherd and his dog to do their thinking for them.

The door suddenly opened and Mrs Charles greeted her with a warm smile. She showed no trace of surprise at the visit and brushed aside Anne Blackmore's insistence that it was getting late and that her husband was sure to be wondering what had become of her; and almost before she realised what was happening to her, Anne Blackmore found herself in Mrs Charles' sitting-room, warming herself by a blazing log fire and drinking the tea which Mrs Charles had seemingly produced out of thin air.

"The jam was delicious," Mrs Blackmore awkwardly attempted to start up a conversation. "It was very kind of you to bring it over to us. I'm sure everyone enjoyed it very much."

Mrs Charles smiled graciously and raised her cup to her lips. The massive diamonds in the rings on her right hand winked mockingly as their facets reflected the flickering firelight. Or so it seemed to Anne Blackmore, who found it an effort to keep her eyes off them.

"The strawberries were excellent last summer," Mrs Charles said chattily. "I managed to achieve a magnificent crop with a minimum of care and attention. I really didn't deserve such good results."

"You enjoy working in the garden?" Mrs Blackmore asked politely.

"No, not really," Mrs Charles smiled. "But with so much land staring one in the face, one feels obliged to make at least a token effort and put it to some use. I can't say that I've ever produced anything from my garden which wouldn't have been considerably cheaper had it been bought in the village. Buying seed is just the beginning—and while today's fertilisers and pest repellants certainly live up to their manufacturers' claims for them, I find them very expensive to buy."

Mrs Blackmore agreed, her eyes lingering momentarily on the glittering necklace round the other woman's throat. Surely not *the* necklace? She looked up into Mrs Charles' deep blue eyes and quickly blinked away her thoughts. Embarrassed colour suffused her neck and face. She was sure that Mrs Charles had been reading her mind and knew exactly what she had been thinking.

'I hear that the village is in the grips of some mystery sickness," Mrs Charles went on to say. "Your husband told me over the telephone the other day that you unfortunately fell victim to it and have been quite gravely ill. I do hope you've completely recovered and are feeling much better now. . . ."

"It was only a gastric upset," Mrs Blackmore protested mildly. "Unpleasant while it lasted, but not serious. A lot more has been made of it than is usual with this type of sickness because with the exception of myself . . . and one other person," she added carefully, colouring a little over her indirect reference to Lionel Preston, "it appears to be confined to quite a large number of the people who have their midday meal at the Council's Day Centre."

Mrs Charles raised her eyebrows a little. "I saw the

'Closed' sign on the door when I went by there today and I wondered what it was all about. . . ."

"The Council has closed it down until their health inspectors have completed their investigations into the cause of the sickness," Mrs Blackmore explained. "I made a sick call on Mrs Hatchard a short while ago—she was taken ill with the same thing—and she told me that Miss Sayer said that the health inspectors aren't at all satisfied with the Day Centre's kitchen facilities: Miss Sayer claims that they're going to insist on radical alterations and renovations to the kitchen to make it easier for the staff to keep clean. Mrs Hatchard said that Miss Sayer seems to think that there's some doubt about whether the Day Center will re-open before the work is carried out."

"One way or another, Margaret Sayer certainly seems to keep her finger well and truly on the pulse of things around the village, doesn't she?" Mrs Charles remarked without any apparent trace of rancour. "I'm sure no one would be half so well informed were it not for her intense interest in the world about her."

"You mustn't mind Miss Sayer—" Mrs Blackmore began, uncomfortably sure that Mrs Charles was referring to the current spate of gossip in the village about herself.

"Oh, I don't, Mrs Blackmore," Mrs Charles gravely interrupted her. "I am, as one would expect of someone in my profession, hypersensitive to the thoughts and feelings of other people, but fortunately quite thick-skinned. What people think and feel about me is their concern, not mine," she smiled thinly.

Abruptly she got up and took Anne Blackmore's cup and saucer from her and placed them on the tray.

"I shall be perfectly frank with you, Mrs Blackmore," she went on after a small pause. "The gift of the strawberry jam was a pretext. I wanted to talk to you. I think you are someone I could trust—"

CHAPTER THIRTEEN

Extremely embarrassed and uncomfortable, Anne Blackmore looked down at her hands and murmured something to the effect that she would hope so.

"My real motive for calling at the vicarage last Wednesday," Mrs Charles then went on to admit, "was that I wanted to talk to you about Henrietta Player. Unfortunately, you were not in. . . ."

Mrs Blackmore nodded, a bewildered expression on her face. "I was over at the Day Centre," she said.

Mrs Charles regarded her thoughtfully for a moment or two, then frowned and said, "If it would not inconvenience you too much, Mrs Blackmore, I would like to have that talk with you about Miss Player now, although first I must have your assurance that for the time being what I wish to discuss with you will go no further than our two selves. . . ."

Mrs Blackmore looked startled, but nevertheless gave the other woman the assurance she sought.

Mrs Charles nodded her satisfaction and said, "I make you the same promise. For the present, this will remain our secret."

Mrs Blackmore frowned, but there was no time to speculate about why Mrs Charles should think it necessary to give her such an assurance. Mrs Charles continued:

"I haven't been completely truthful with the police, Mrs Blackmore— No, perhaps that's being a little harsh on myself. Let me put it another way. . . . When I was interviewed by the police shortly after Miss Player was murdered, I wasn't as frank and open with them as I might've been: I didn't tell them that I had once been summoned by Miss Player, invited into Whitethatch Cottage to examine the contents of several bottles of liquor which she claimed had been tampered with by you."

Mrs Blackmore's bottom jaw dropped and for a very long moment she stared open-mouthed at the other woman. "That's absolutely preposterous!" she finally spluttered. "I have always been strictly teetotal. You can ask my husband . . . anyone!"

The diamond rings winked tantalisingly at her as Mrs Charles raised her hands in a gesture of restraint. "Please hear me out, Mrs Blackmore," she asked. "Do not alarm yourself. This is, as I said a moment ago, just between the two of us. You know, of course, the occasion to which I refer?"

Mrs Blackmore gave her a bleak look. "I can guess. The day you and I passed one another on the road as I was on my way back to the vicarage after visiting Miss Player. I thought you were paying her a visit, too," she finished, wide-eyed.

"No—I was on my way to see Mr Forbes, who was ill in bed with the 'flu at the time: but as I was walking past Miss Player's gate, she suddenly appeared at her front door and beckoned frantically to me. She looked quite distraught, and I naturally thought that she had been taken suddenly ill and was calling for assistance. However, nothing could have been further from the truth. She was certainly greatly distressed, but not about herself. She took me into her sitting-room and showed me several bottles of spirits, the level of which she claimed she discovered to be greatly reduced every time you left after visiting her."

"I never touched them!" Mrs Blackmore declared hotly. "I didn't even know that she kept liquor on the premises. And what about all those vagrants she allowed to come and go as they pleased? How could she be so sure who touched the bottles?"

"Exactly," Mrs Charles said evenly. "Which has set me thinking. What if I misunderstood Miss Player that day and she wasn't talking about you?"

"But you said—" Mrs Blackmore began fractiously.

"Yes, yes," the other woman said soothingly. "I know what I said . . . and no one would blame me for mistakenly thinking that the *she* Miss Player referred to was you, the person I had just seen leaving her cottage."

"You mean she didn't actually refer to me by name?"

"No. Miss Player simply said that the bottles of spirits were tampered with every time that *she* came round. Now who was I to think she meant—some fictional being, the creation of a demented imagination, or the woman I had seen with her minutes earlier?"

Mrs Blackmore closed her eyes tightly and gasped for air. She had come over quite giddy and faint.

"Are you all right, my dear?" Mrs Charles asked concernedly. She quickly went over to her and placed a hand on the shoulder of Mrs Blackmore's thick white polo-neck sweater which felt surprisingly damp to the touch, as if it had been directly exposed to the atmosphere. Either that or the raincoat that she had been wearing when she had arrived afforded little protection against the kind of weather that they had had that day, which would not have surprised Mrs Charles in the least. The garment in question was, in her opinion, much too modish to be functional, a

fault which Mrs Charles found with so much of today's off-the-peg clothing.

Beneath the gentle pressure of her hand, Mrs
Charles could feel the tension of the other woman's
shoulder and neck muscles. "Try to relax, Mrs
Blackmore," she said quietly. "Let go of those
muscles: you're strangling your lungs. You must give
yourself a chance to breathe. . . ."

Mrs Blackmore's shoulders sagged in response to
the gentle persuasion in the other woman's voice and
in a little while her breathing became less stertorous
and colour began to return to her face.

"I'm sorry," she apologised at length, pushing her
hair back from her face with the side of her hand. "I
feel such a fool—I'm not normally the fainting type.
It's just that . . . what you said . . . it's come as
a bit of a shock. Nobody's ever accused me of anything like that before."

"I'm quite sure they haven't, my dear," Mrs
Charles quietly reassured her. She paused for a moment, then took her hand away and went back to the
sofa and sat down again.

"Could there have been anyone else, some other
woman, there in the cottage while you were with Miss
Player that day?" she went on to ask, a small frown
creasing her brow. "I went no further than the sitting-room with her, but I certainly didn't get the
feeling that there was someone else about the place,
and I'm usually sensitive to these things. But that is
not to say that there hadn't been some other person
there moments earlier, someone who left by the back
door and quickly disappeared across the fields, either
while you were taking your leave of Miss Player, or as
she was calling out to me."

"Someone from the village?" Mrs Blackmore mused
out loud.

Mrs Charles did not hurry her deliberations.

"But *who*?" Mrs Blackmore asked abruptly, her thin, pencilled-in eyebrows arched interrogatively.

"I don't know," Mrs Charles replied, slowly shaking her head. "But if my suspicion is correct and someone else was there while you were visiting Miss Player . . . someone from the village who deliberately kept out of sight because she knew that you would recognise her . . . it could explain why Miss Player simply said *she* and expected me to know to whom she referred."

Mrs Blackmore was nodding thoughtfully. "It is possible, I suppose, but—" She hesitated, after a moment guardedly continuing:

"I think I'd be more inclined to say that she was suffering from delusions. She'd been a little strange for some time . . . I mean more so than usual. I used to call round to see her about twice a month . . . every other week if I could manage it . . . and I suppose it would've been approximately six months before she was murdered that I first noticed something different, changed, about her. I thought she was finally going mad . . ." Mrs Blackmore confessed a little self-consciously.

"Or someone was slowly driving her out of her mind." Mrs Charles spoke so quietly that the other woman missed most of what she said.

"It was nothing," Mrs Charles replied absently when asked to repeat herself. "I was just remembering out loud something that I once saw happen to someone many years ago." She frowned a little. "What about this man who was seen hanging about the cottage a few days before Miss Player's body was found? You were one of those who saw him, weren't you?"

"David Sayer seemed to think so. But not on the

Friday, the day the police said Miss Player was murdered. It was several months earlier. He was rather an unpleasant sort of person," Mrs Blackmore remarked reflectively. "Very aggressive . . . had a massive chip on his shoulder about something—his affliction, most probably. He couldn't talk properly . . . I don't mean that he was subnormal . . . mentally defective: my feeling was that he would've been a lot sharper than most. I'm not sure, but I think he had a cleft palate. David Sayer said that that anonymous phone call the police had . . . the man who rang and told them that Miss Player was dead?" She widened her eyes interrogatively and Mrs Charles gave a quick nod. "He also had a speech impediment. . . ."

"Yes, I heard all about it at the time from Mr Forbes," Mrs Charles said thoughtfully. "Quite obviously one and the same person. . . . How were you able to get into conversation with him?"

"He was at the cottage one day when I called round to see Miss Player—and judging by the way that he spoke to her, it wasn't his first visit, either. He was very rude to her . . . why she put up with it, I don't know: I certainly wouldn't have. I would've sent him packing!"

"Perhaps she was afraid of him?" Mrs Charles suggested.

"She might've been. It's hard to say now: it was so long ago. But I don't think I thought so at the time." Mrs Blackmore paused and stroked her hair, something she did frequently—out of nervous habit, Mrs Charles was inclined to think.

Still stroking her hair, Mrs Blackmore went on:

"Miss Player did tend to be a bit on the timid side. She was the sort of person . . . well, the kind who could easily be intimidated by someone with a more forceful personality. This might've been why she avoided becoming involved in any way with us, the villagers. She wasn't a particularly mentally alert person. I found her rather vague, slow-witted. But she certainly wasn't malicious." Mrs Blackmore coloured heavily at the recollection of the charge which Miss Player had allegedly laid against her. She paused momentarily, her hand held against the side of her head. Then, curiously: "What did you say to her about the missing alcohol?"

"What could I say? I suspected that the poor thing had been drinking it herself and that her memory was playing tricks on her, so I soothed her down a bit and suggested that in future she should keep the bottles in some place which could be kept securely locked; but she claimed that it wouldn't make any difference . . . she said it didn't matter what she hid away, *she* always found everything in the end."

Mrs Blackmore stared hard at Mrs Charles and reddened. "What did she mean by that?" she asked defensively.

"I didn't ask, but I assumed she meant that this other woman was in the habit of going through the cottage every time she called on her to see what she could find."

Mrs Blackmore was too appalled by Mrs Charles' assumption to say anything at all in her own defence. She simply stared wide-eyed and slack-mouthed at the older woman and waited for her to go on.

"Did Miss Player ever have another visitor or visitors on any of the other occasions on which you visited her?" Mrs Charles asked. "Someone other than the man with the speech impediment?"

Mrs Blackmore shook her head numbly. "No one I was ever aware of. There could've been someone out in the kitchen or in one of the other rooms, I suppose. It was such a long time ago," she finished, a trace of exasperation in her voice.

"Never mind. It was a slim hope."

"I don't understand, Mrs Charles. These questions . . . what are you hoping to prove?"

"Why, that I didn't murder Henrietta Player, of course!"

Anne Blackmore coloured deeply and was about to profess that that was the last thing that anyone thought. She was deterred by the expression in the other woman's eyes. Whatever else Edwina Charles might be, she was no fool.

CHAPTER FOURTEEN

A short while after passing the Blackmores on the road to the village that morning, Cyril Forbes had boarded the ten forty-five train from Gidding to Waterloo. At one thirty in the afternoon, he was sitting on a damp wooden bench in a small square near the Old Vic. He was still sitting on the bench an hour later, alone and very cold and quite certain in his own mind that Elaina Petrovic, who had agreed to act as intermediary for the purposes of attempting to recover the painting which his sister was sure had been stolen from the sitting-room of Whitethatch Cottage, had been duped into believing that the *Player*'s new owner was willing to show his face and run the risk that there had never been any connection between the person with whom he had professed an eagerness to do business and the artist's murdered daughter.

There were a few other people about—two middle-aged down-and-outs almost conspiratorially sharing a loaf of bread, one of whom had begged five pence from Cyril Forbes moments after he had sat down; a man of about thirty-five, fair-haired and wearing faded blue jeans and with very red, slightly swollen hands, asleep on a bench on his own; and, on the next bench along from him, another man of about the same age in dirty mustard-coloured velvet cords

and a thick dark brown woolen sweater over which
he wore a heavily embroidered, grease-stained goat-
skin coat with a long, matted fringe of off-white goat-
hair. A green knitted cap was pulled well down over
his ears, almost to his eyes.

All four men had appeared more or less at the
same time, and at length Cyril Forbes made up his
mind between *Red Hands* and *Goat-skin Coat*. It had
to be one or the other . . . *Red Hands,* Cyril
Forbes thought; and in view of the gathering clouds,
which had darkened the sky considerably in the last
five or so minutes (and firmly convinced that the
longer that he remained in London the greater the
risk of being waylaid by Elaina Petrovic!), he decided
to put his powers of deduction to the test. He made
an elaborate pretence of looking at the time, then got
up and walked briskly towards Waterloo Road. As no
direct approach had been made, he expected to be
followed. And he was . . . by the man in the goat-
skin coat.

Without once having looked behind him since leaving the bench in the little square, Cyril Forbes
boarded the three fifty-five from Waterloo. He left the
train an hour later at Gidding and hurried out to the
station car park to collect his motor-cycle. As he was
pulling down the visor on his crash helmet, he felt a
hand on his shoulder.

"I think," mumbled the man in the goat-skin coat,
"that *take me to your leader* would be appropriate
right now, don't you?"

"I thought it was the other fellow," was all Cyril
Forbes said. He climbed on to the bike and the other
man mounted the pillion.

Mrs Charles opened the door and stared past her
brother at the man who was standing behind him.

Minutes earlier she had said goodbye to Anne Blackmore, and she half-expected to see her back again for some reason. Mrs Charles glanced along the road, but there was no sign of either Anne Blackmore or her car. Both had gone.

Cyril Forbes stepped inside and quickly disappeared behind a closed door at the other end of the hall.

The man in the goat-skin coat studied Mrs Charles' face closely. His own face was unpleasant—gaunt, unshaven. Strands of greasy fair hair fell lankly to his shoulders from beneath the knitted cap and mingled with the goat-hair fringe round the neck of his coat.

"What's your game, missus?" he muttered at length, very indistinctly and with some difficulty as he had a pronounced speech defect. He had looked at first puzzled, but now something like mistrust was showing in his weak blue eyes. "You're—" He broke off and looked round quickly as Cyril Forbes kick-started his motor-cycle and roared off into the night.

It was a minute or so before anyone spoke. The motor-cycle could still be heard zooming back towards the motorway.

"May I suggest that you step inside where it is a little warmer?"

At the sound of her voice, the man turned back to Mrs Charles and his eyes lighted hungrily on the necklace round her throat. His thin, cruel mouth twisted into a hard smile and he inclined his head at the hall. "You got someone else in there? The police maybe?"

"No—I am on my own: you have nothing to fear from me."

He considered the possibility that she was not telling him the truth and while he thought it unlikely, nevertheless decided to make sure. He brushed roughly past her and went to the door through which Cyril Forbes had disappeared. The door opened into the kitchen, beyond which was a further door which gave on to the garden.

He turned back and then disappeared down a short passage to the left of the hall. Mrs Charles heard first the bathroom door, then one of the two bedrooms open and close. A few moments later, the man reappeared.

"Satisfied?" she enquired. With her heavily-ringed right hand, she indicated that she wished him to precede her into the sitting-room.

He looked her up and down contemptuously. These rich old ducks were all the same—they asked for all they got!

The curtains in the room had not been drawn, which made him feel exposed and vulnerable, and he moved quickly to remedy the matter.

"I shouldn't if I were you," Mrs Charles advised him quietly. "My brother might think there is something wrong."

"Eh?" he said thickly, his right hand tugging at the cretonne drapery.

"Those curtains are my means of communicating with him that all is not well. Tonight, of course, he will be watching them a little more closely than usual: in fact, now that he has reached his home and has me safely in his sights, should either you or I disappear from view for as much as a second, he'll become most alarmed and telephone a certain police superintendent who was very much involved in a murder enquiry that was conducted here some years ago."

There was a long silence, then the man narrowed his eyes thoughtfully at her. "Your brother? Not that dozy bit of work who led me straight to you?" he sneered.

Her only response was a very small smile which he found somewhat unnerving.

"What sort of mug d'you take me for?" he croaked, blustering a little. "He must live miles away from here—"

Mrs Charles was still smiling. "A good five to ten minutes' walk at least from poor Miss Player's cottage . . . in the direction of the motorway. My brother's house is the one with the rather unusual wireless aerial in the front garden—you must have passed it many times . . . not recently, of course, but back in the days when Henrietta Player was alive and you used to be one of her visitors."

He studied her, after a long moment again narrowing his eyes, this time maliciously. "What's your brother got, lady—extra-sensory perception?"

"No, nothing like that. A particularly high-powered telescope. He keeps it in his attic . . . not just to keep an eye on me, you understand: he is expecting a visitor, a certain gentleman from outer space whose acquaintance he made some years ago. They met one Wednesday, out in the fields . . . over by the motorway."

The man clearly believed that she was mad, but was just as clearly unsure about the telescope and the threat concerning the police. The feeling that mad or not she was telling the truth sent icy chills down his spine, and he released the curtain and edged nervously towards the door.

"You don't really have any alternative, you know," Mrs Charles told him gravely. "Either you co-operate and give me the information I want or my brother will contact the police. And let me assure you that you won't get away so easily this time. . . ."

He became sullen. "There's nothing I could tell you that you'd want to know."

"Let me be the judge of that. Now . . . shall we sit down?" Her inviting smile extended no further than her lips. Her eyes were cold and hard and left him in no doubt that this was a very determined woman, one who wouldn't take no for an answer.

He glanced at the window and then morosely came back into the centre of the room and lowered himself woodenly into the straight-backed chair which had been favoured the previous Wednesday by ex-Detective Chief Superintendent Sayer. He folded his arms across his stomach and stared gloomily at them.

"Just once—" he began in a barely intelligible mutter which, when he continued, was punctuated by a particularly pungent laugh. "I sat there listening to them talk about the painting you want. 'Robert, my friend,' I said to myself, 'it's finally happened. Your luck's changed. This time you can't go wrong. . . .'" He lapsed into a sulky silence.

"You didn't actually see any of my advertisements yourself?" Mrs Charles enquired, and realised immediately what a ridiculous thing that was to ask. Of course he hadn't seen them. His life-style hadn't altered a jot over the past six years: he was still living rough, rootless as ever, wandering from place to place. Such a man wouldn't be in the habit of keeping abreast of current events through the medium of the newspapers, let alone read the Personal columns!

He was shaking his head. "I heard about it from some friends . . . flat-mates of mine," he added and laughed. It was an ugly, bitter sound which hung heavily on the silence that followed. Then he shrugged. "They're not really friends. I haven't any. And we're not flat-mates neither. Squatters . . . that's what they call us down at the Town Hall. The lot of us moved into this condemned house in Islington on the same day a couple of weeks back. They're all artists . . . a couple aren't bad neither. One of them knew about your advert. through some friends of his who run an art gallery. I couldn't believe my ears at first: it just seemed too good to be true; but then the next day I checked with a couple of newspaper offices and sure enough, one of them had the advert. all right."

"Were you telling the truth? Do you still have the painting that you stole from Henrietta Player's cottage?"

"I could hardly get rid of it, could I?" he said haltingly. "I expected that they'd catch whoever killed the old girl, and then after all the fuss and commotion had died down, I reckoned that I could start thinking about selling it. After all, it's not as though I didn't have a right to it. She was my old lady."

CHAPTER FIFTEEN

Mrs Charles was frowning. "Am I to understand that Henrietta Player was your mother?"

He shrugged his shoulders irritably. "She never denied it."

"You're not sure?" she asked, rounding her eyes at him.

"No!" he snapped. Then, after a small pause, and with a long sigh, he added: "Sure enough. I went back and got it out of the old witch who used to run the orphanage that I was dumped in when my mother, dear sweet Henrietta, found out that I couldn't talk like other people."

"Are you quite sure that that was the reason?" Mrs Charles asked, recalling Edward Player's reputed abhorrence of children—one who was imperfect and apparently illegitimate more than most?—and that Henrietta Player, his only child, had nursed him devotedly, though perhaps not quite so willingly as one might previously have thought, for many years prior to his death.

He snarled at Mrs Charles like a cowed dog. "What other reason could there be?"

She raised her eyebrows a little and made no comment. Her thoughts on his grandfather and his mother were, after all, pure speculation: there could have been many other reasons why his mother had been unable to raise him herself.

"When did you take the *Player*?" she asked. "Was it before or after you found your mother's body?"

He turned his head on one side and squinted at her. "What makes you think I didn't kill the old girl?"

The very direct way in which Mrs Charles was looking at him made him feel nervous, on edge. He looked away from her and rushed on:

"I wanted to—that's why I went there in the first place . . . after I'd found out who I really was."

"What stopped you?"

His bitter laugh was more of an ugly croak. "She was even more pathetic than I am—weak, sponged off. Not worth the effort. I was sorry that I wasted my time. I wished I'd never gone near her."

"But you went back a second time," Mrs Charles reminded him evenly. "Why? To steal the *Player*?"

He shrugged again. "Like I said: she owed me something. And at the rate things seemed to be going, she would've been picked clean in no time. That woman really had her hooks into her."

"No doubt you are referring now to the person whom you expected to find when you came here tonight with my brother," Mrs Charles remarked.

He nodded. "I thought she'd gone to ground, like me, and that the advertisement in the paper meant that she'd decided that it was now safe to try and get the *Player*. I was pretty sure that she knew who'd taken it: I'd be very surprised if the old lady didn't tell her all about me . . . she would've had that wrung out of her for sure." He grimaced. "You'd think that just once I'd get lucky, wouldn't you? A first-class ticket for life," he went on grimly. "That was what I had all worked out for myself. No more scrounging . . ."

"Blackmail?" Mrs Charles' tone was mildly disapproving.

"So?" he said sharply, his eyes cold and defensive. "You haven't told me what you want yet," he reminded her.

"Who was she . . . this woman whom you mentioned a moment ago?" Mrs Charles asked.

"I don't know. I only got a proper look at her the once, the first time I went to the cottage to see the old lady. She came in while I was talking to the old girl and I could see right away that there was something funny going on between the two of them. Henrietta was scared stiff of her—at least, she acted as if she was. Anyway, I hung about the place for a bit and then when I got fed up with waiting for this woman to go, I wandered off."

"Can you remember what your mother and this woman talked about?"

"Nothing much while I was there. But didn't I get an earful after they thought I'd gone?" he smirked. "The old girl had obviously been giving this woman money, and she wanted more. Henrietta said there wasn't any, it had all gone. She was sort of whimpering when she said it . . . as if the other woman had hit her, or was threatening to . . . I was crouching outside the living-room window: I couldn't see what was going on. Then the other woman said something about the money under the floorboards, and Henrietta told her that there wasn't any and never had been and that she could look for herself and see. Something like that . . ." His voice tailed off into a thoughtful silence. Then after a while, he went on:

"She—the other woman—said something about a

church . . . something about a donation," he frowned. "I wasn't sure what it was all about . . . whether she wanted a donation or the old lady had given one . . . I couldn't hear all that well, and the other woman was angry and speaking very fast. Then it all went quiet and after a bit I took a quick look through the window, but I couldn't see anyone: they'd both disappeared . . . so I slipped round to the back of the cottage—and there she was . . . this woman . . . nipping across the fields as fast as her two little legs would carry her. I went inside and found the old lady in the hall talking to someone else, some other woman. I stayed around for a while and then I got cheesed off with it all and left—"

Mrs Charles nodded thoughtfully. Then she frowned at him. "Was that the last time that you saw your mother alive?"

"Yes and no. She was alive enough two or three months later . . . when I went back for the *Player* . . . but I didn't actually see her. I could only hear her talking . . . her and that other woman—the one who was bullying her. They were in the living-room together . . . where the *Player* was hanging; so I decided to leave and go back for it later . . . when the old lady was on her own. I didn't particularly want any outside witnesses to the fact that I'd been about the place, especially if old Henrietta took it into her head to report the theft of the *Player*—and me, her darling little boy!—to the police. I didn't really think she would . . . she was much too timid for anything like that . . . but I wasn't taking any chances."

"I understand that there were a number of other paintings hanging elsewhere in the cottage: why didn't you settle for one of them instead? I heard that they were all valuable."

"Not as valuable as the one in the living-room," he smiled crookedly. "I looked up some art books on Henrietta's old man after I found out who I was, and *The Brewery* was supposed to be one of the best examples of his post-something or other period—and nobody seemed to know where it was . . . what had become of it . . . a very strong point in its favour as far as I was concerned. One of the books that I got hold of put it in a private art collection in New York—"

Mrs Charles was nodding. "Yes, I made some enquiries myself after I spotted it on Miss Player's sitting-room wall one day. I have always been interested in art, particularly that of Edward Player's period, and I thought I recognized it. My information was as vague as yours . . . that *The Brewery* was thought to be somewhere in America, which convinced me that it was still in this country . . . in the possession of the artist's daughter . . . and that it was the painting that I had seen hanging in her sitting-room." She paused for a moment. Then: "I wonder why Miss Player's over-bearing lady-friend showed no interest in it . . . or in any of the other paintings in the cottage?"

"She knew what she was doing," he said dryly. "Anybody can get rid of stolen cash and jewellery without too much sweat. But well-known works of art—" He shook his head slowly and made a face. "You've got to have the connections. . . ."

"The last time you went to the cottage . . . did you hear any of her conversation with Miss Player?"

"A little. . . . The woman was angry . . . and I mean *angry!*" he said with a fierce look. "She kept threatening the old girl that it was her last chance to tell her where the cash was hidden. . . ." He shrugged a little and gave a sigh.

"When I went back a couple of hours later—I had a kip in the garden-shed while I was waiting for her to go—the old lady was dead." He looked down at his scuffed boots and frowned. "You know, when you live rough like me, you see some pretty grisly sights and you soon get hardened to them; but that old lady . . . that was something else again. She . . . that woman . . . must've been mad, right off her chump, to do what she did to that poor old girl!"

"You were responsible for the pebbles that were found near your mother's body, weren't you?" Mrs Charles asked kindly.

He nodded morosely and continued to gaze at his boots. "I dunno—seeing the poor old girl like that . . . I must've gone a bit soft in the head or something," he said gruffly. "I mean . . . what did I care about her? She never cared nothing for me!"

"Making up a formation of pebbles similar to Widow Roth's Stones was your way of telling the police that the person who had murdered your mother was someone from the village, wasn't it?" she said gently.

He shrugged his shoulders again and looked annoyed, irritated perhaps by what he now considered had been a moment's weakness on his part. Then he sighed as if he were finally prepared to accept that he was no match for this shrewdly observant woman.

"The first time I went to the cottage I passed some men who were working in a field near them . . . those stones," he explained. "They were scientists of some kind or other, and I asked the old lady what they were up to out there, and she told me all that rubbish the villagers believe about Widow Roth and witchcraft. I didn't think it was the sort of thing too many outsiders would know and so I reckoned that if I did something like it . . . laid out some stones like Widow Roth's near the old lady's body . . . it was sure to set the police on the right track. I thought they'd catch up with that woman in no time. But nothing ever happened. She got away with murder and I got lumbered with a painting that was too hot for anyone to handle."

"Can you describe this woman to me?"

He shook his head. "I guess I'd know her if I saw her again, but don't ask me to tell you what she looked like. She was just a woman . . . you know—" He broke off and thoughtfully stroked the ribbed turn-back on his cap. "There is something I remember. . . . Her hair."

CHAPTER SIXTEEN

"Well?" Frank Blackmore smiled across at his wife. "How much did it cost?"

Anne Blackmore had been gazing absently at the rather cheerless fire which for want of a little care and attention was slowly dying in the grate, but she looked up sharply as her husband spoke. "How much did what cost?" she asked, puzzled by his question.

"Whatever it was that took your eye today," he said, still smiling. "I know that look on your face. Shoes, hat, coat, dress? What was it? *Jewellery?*" His eyebrows were raised interrogatively over an expression of gentle amusement.

She did not return his smile and looked back at the hearth. "You know I didn't go into Gidding today," she replied, getting up to put another log on the fire. "I didn't dare—you made enough fuss about the little that I did do."

Her tone was a trifle short which was unusual and so very unlike her that her husband was moved to wonder if she had been over-exerting herself.

"You're quite sure you're feeling all right again, dear?" he asked her concernedly.

"Of course I'm all right," she replied, looking round at him in surprise as she stroked some life into the fire.

He studied her for a moment. He was inclined to

think that she was not telling him the truth. Her hair, perhaps because of its deep, rich, natural colour, had always been a very accurate barometer of her health and noticeably lacked its usual healthy lustre and shine.

"I went to see Mrs Charles today," she remarked as she returned to her chair.

"I know, dear," he said, frowning a little. "You told me." He paused. Then: "You've got something on your mind, haven't you? Something is worrying you."

"No," she said, and turned her head abruptly away so that the flush of guilty colour which she could feel inching its way up her neck towards her face would be less apparent to him. "I was just thinking about those diamonds," she went on quickly. "Father would've called them instruments of the devil, indisputable proof of his, the devil's, existence. He would've said that they would bring evil down on all who looked on them. . . ."

"To which period of enlightenment can we attribute those particular pears of wisdom?" he asked dryly.

There was a small silence. Then Anne sighed and smiled gravely at him.

"Well, there you are," he smiled back. "That answers it, doesn't it?"

"I wasn't asking a question. It was meant to be a statement." She hesitated, then thoughtfully added: "It was true, though, what he said . . . wasn't it?"

"Nonsense," her husband replied, puzzled by her mood which was completely out of character. He could not remember ever having seen her like this before, so depressed and introspective.

"No," she said strangely. "It's not nonsense, Frank. And you know it isn't. For as far back as I can remember, Father went every Sunday to Hyde Park Corner to preach the sins of materialism . . . then there were those sabbaticals of his when he would vanish from our lives—Mother's and mine—while he roamed the countryside spreading the word . . . and then finally," she sighed again, "there came the time when we realised that we weren't ever going to see him again . . . Mother was told that he'd found himself a rich widow lady to keep him in the manner to which he wished to grow accustomed. So you see," she frowned earnestly at the fire, "Father proved his point, the point he'd been making all those years about the evils of hankering after the material things in life. He looked on his rich widow and saw her fine jewels and furs, and the temptation was too great, too great even for him . . . a man of *his* firm beliefs and convictions."

"The latent alcoholic is often the most ardent prohibitionist," her husband remarked with a small sigh. "Whatever your father became he was to begin with—I doubt if he realised it, but all those Sunday afternoon sermons of his were really directed at himself . . . for his own benefit."

"That's what I can't get out of my mind. I try very hard to keep a sense of proportion about it, but it's something that has been worrying me for a long time," she admitted after a short pause. "I'm afraid that with very little encouragement at all I could become very materialistic. . . ."

"Why? Because you like and appreciate beautiful things?" her husband queried. "Since when has that been a sin?"

"When the liking and appreciating becomes coveting," she replied quietly. "*Envy* of what others have which you yourself would like to possess—the non-essential things like, well, like having masses of expensive jewellery . . . all the things that you know there isn't one chance in a million that you are ever likely to be able to afford to buy."

He smiled at her affectionately. "Which of Mrs Charles' little trinkets do you covet and envy her for, my pet? One of those remarkable rings of hers?"

"No: I've told you what I think of them," she said shortly. "Only she could wear them: on anyone else they would look extremely vulgar."

"Well, then, where is the problem?" he grinned.

"She was wearing the Stuart necklace this afternoon," she said oddly.

"The Stuart necklace?" he repeated with a frown.

"The diamond necklace that Mr Preston—Cissie Keith's cousin—said belonged to that woman everyone in the village seems to think Mrs Charles murdered. At least," she added after a slight pause, "I *think* it was the Stuart necklace. It was as though Mrs Charles knew my weakness, Frank—" she frowned at him. "As though she's spotted the flaw in my character which I've inherited from my father, and was deliberately tempting me with that necklace."

He studied her for a moment without comment. Then, very lightly, he said, "Well, you know what I always say about temptation, my love. Give in to it!"

"I'd rather you were anything but flippant about something as serious as I feel this is, Frank," she said, and he was amazed to see her eyes fill with tears. "I'm frightened . . . I can't help thinking that this afternoon while I was visiting Mrs Charles I took a long look at myself in a mirror and saw right through to the other side . . . to the dark evil side of myself."

Frank Blackmore left his chair and went over and sat on the arm-rest of hers. He took her hand in his. It felt hot and when he lightly brushed several stray strands of hair from her face, her forehead too was hot, although there was no sign of feverishness in her colour. She was very pale and there were dark smudges beneath her eyes.

"From time to time we all have our doubts and fears about ourselves, Anne," he said quietly. "And it's only to be expected that every now and again we'll be confronted with situations which will recall painful memories of things that have happened to us at one time or another in the past. In your case, your painful memories are all associated with your father, and when confronted with a situation which brings them flooding back to you, you feel all over again the terrible hurt and shame that you suffered because of his actions; and then, out of this hurt and shame comes the fear that you yourself will one day cause the same pain and anguish to the people closest to you. It's only a fear Anne: a silly, groundless fear with no basis in reality."

She looked up at him for a very long moment. Did he really understand what she was trying to tell him? He was a good man . . . kind, understanding, but most of the time, she felt, inclined to exist on some ethereal plane where everybody wandered about contentedly in baggy trousers and ill-fitting jackets, and people were every bit as good if not better than himself. How then could he expect her to be reassured? She simply couldn't believe that there had ever been anything in his own life that could be compared with the cross which she had to bear. She sighed again: then, wearily, she said:

"Are you sure that's all it is, Frank?"

"Positive," he said cheerfully. "Now, you didn't tell me . . . what did you and Mrs Charles find to talk about this afternoon?"

She was quiet for a moment, then she closed her eyes and rested her head against the back of her chair. "Oh, you know . . . nothing much," she said. "The usual things: the garden . . ."

Cissie Keith opened her front door and said, "Oh . . . it's you: I was hoping it was Lionel. You haven't seen him, have you?" she went on worriedly, peering round her visitor at the black, wet night.

Margaret Sayer shook herself and her umbrella like a wet, shaggy dog, stamped her small feet on the mat and then stepped into the tiny hall and removed her coat. Meanwhile, Cissie Keith had continued:

"Lionel went out this afternoon and he hasn't come back yet. I don't know what to do. Do you think I should ring the police? He might've had an accident."

"What? Hasn't he been back since he went over to see Mrs Charles?" Miss Sayer demanded, handing her coat to Cissie Keith who hung it up on a peg beside one of her own.

"He didn't say anything to me about going to see Mrs Charles." Cissie Keith frowned, waiting with out-stretched hand for Miss Sayer to remove her hat. "He said he was going for a walk over to the motorway."

"And you believed him!" The long pin which Miss Sayer viciously stabbed into her hat heavily punctuated what was more of a stinging remark than an actual question.

The other woman's eyes were so big and round that they seemed to take up most of her face. "Mrs Charles would be the last person on earth that Lionel would ever want to see again. I can't think of anything that he would want to say to her: he feels just like you do about her."

Miss Sayer swept through to her friend's small sitting-room and sat down on the sofa. "Are you quite sure that he's told you all there is to know about himself and Mrs Charles?" she asked peremptorily.

Cissie Keith looked at her anxiously. "What do you mean?"

"It's beginning to seem to me that there could be a whole lot more to his story about her than you and I are ever likely to know, my girl."

"Oh, no, Margaret: you're wrong there. Lionel would *never* keep anything from me."

"We'll see," Miss Sayer said darkly.

"I wish you wouldn't say things like that to me, Margaret," Cissie Keith said with a vexed frown. "You're making me feel very nervous and upset: it's bad enough that he hasn't come home, without you making all these horrible insinuations. . . ." She looked round anxiously at the hall. "I do wish he'd hurry up and come back. I really feel quite sick with worry."

"Oh, for goodness' sake!" Miss Sayer exclaimed. "He's a grown man, not a little boy . . . and if he's all you're going to talk about, I'm beginning to wish I'd stayed where I was!"

"Why did you come round?" Cissie Keith asked curiously. "You don't usually go out after dark on your own."

An oily shine on Margaret Sayer's hooded lids, accentuated by inadequate lighting, gave her an almost sinister appearance around the eyes.

"I just wanted to see for myself that you were still in the land of the living," she said carelessly.

"I'm still far from well," Cissie Keith fervently assured her. "I dropped right off to sleep after Lionel went out this afternoon and I only woke up a short while ago. That's *very* unusual for me," she said fretfully. "I don't expect that I'll be able to sleep tonight now: I never can when I have a rest during the day."

She looked at the clock on the mantelshelf and did some mental arithmetic. "Lionel's been gone over five hours. . . . Whatever can he be doing all this time? I wonder if Mrs Blackmore would know?" She frowned. "They did leave here together. . . . Do you think I should ring her?"

"What was she doing here today?" Miss Sayer asked suspiciously.

"She called round to see if I was feeling any better."

Miss Sayer made an exasperated clicking sound with her tongue. "My goodness me, my girl: it wouldn't do for you to be *really* sick, would it? All this fuss and to-do . . . anyone would think you were lying at death's door!" The hooded lids drooped with disapproval as she gazed thoughtfully at the other woman.

After a very long moment, Miss Sayer looked away: then, inching forward on the sofa, she peered at the fashion model on the cover of the magazine which was lying on the occasional table. A patch of scalp on the crown of Margaret Sayer's head, about the size of a ten-pence piece, showed pink and bare. She had been cutting her hair herself again.

"Why do you think Lionel went over to see Mrs Charles?" she asked without looking up.

"I keep telling you, Margaret," Cissie Keith said on a note of hysteria. "He *didn't* go to see her: he simply went for a walk."

There was a sudden rush of noise somewhere outside and Cissie Keith stiffened and listened intently until everything went quiet with the closing of the front door of a neighbouring cottage.

"Oh, well . . ." Miss Sayer said, abruptly pushing the magazine aside. "If this is all the sense I'm going to get out of you tonight, I'm off back home. I'm sorry I bothered!"

She stood up.

"No, don't go," Cissie Keith pleaded with her. "I'll put the kettle on . . . we'll have a cup of tea. But I do think I should ring the police," she said, quite loudly but to herself as she forestalled any argument that might have been forthcoming by hurrying out to the kitchen. "It's not like Lionel, not a bit like him. . . ."

CHAPTER SEVENTEEN

Cyril Forbes was sitting well forward on the sofa with his hands clasped loosely round his knees. His dark eyes were alert and darted about inquisitively, following his sister as she moved back and forth between the china cabinet and the small, round dining-table on which she was setting out her superb collection of Victorian Staffordshire portrait figures. The fact that tomorrow was a Wednesday largely accounted for Cyril Forbes' present animation, but there was something else on his mind, and his sister waited patiently for it to bubble to the surface.

"There's something going on in the village, 'Del," he said as she drew out a chair and sat down at the table. "There was a police car outside Miss Sayer's cottage and another one parked near Mrs Keith's. Nobody I talked to seemed to know what's going on, but I think they've lost someone."

Mrs Charles gave her brother a bemused look and then took up a soft cloth and concentrated all her attention on the mostly white and gold porcelaneous figures of the 19th-century American actresses, Charlotte and Susan Cushman as Romeo and Juliet, one of the creations of the 'Tallis' potter, Thomas arr.

"Who do you think has gone missing?" she asked at length. "Cecilia Keith? Margaret Sayer?" she eyed him quizzically. "Surely not the both of them?"

He didn't give her a direct reply. He went on:

"There are police and dogs in the fields . . . you know, behind Whitethatch Cottage."

"Whatever for?" she exclaimed, putting down the duster and transferring her full attention to him.

"It's like when that Superintendent fellow—Sayer—was spying on me," he told her. "They're wandering around and poking about in the grass as if they're looking for something."

"How very peculiar," she murmured thoughtfully. "I wonder if one of the children from the village is missing—?"

"I was watching them early this morning," he continued. "They started out over by the motorway, and it looks to me as if they could be working their way here."

"Perhaps I should run along out to the kitchen and put the kettle on," she said dryly. "If you're right, we could be about to have visitors." She took up the cloth again, staring absently at it for a moment or two before carrying on with the dusting of her collection.

"That fellow I brought here last night . . . did he tell you what you wanted to know?" her brother asked after a slight pause.

There was a long silence. Then Mrs Charles put down the duster and rested her arms lightly on the table. When she spoke, her tone was grave.

"I think," she said, "I know who killed Janet Stuart."

"Was it the same person who murdered Miss Player?" he asked imperturbably.

"Yes," she replied. "However, I'm going to need some rather specialised help to prove it."

"Me again?" he enquired, a little anxiously. He

hoped his sister hadn't forgotten that tomorrow was Wednesday.

"No, not this time, Cyril," she said slowly. "It was rather odd that you should bring up Superintendent Sayer's name—"

"Him? You're not going to ask *him* to help you?"

"Yes, Cyril," she nodded. "As a matter of fact, that is exactly what I intend to do. I was trying to telephone him just before you arrived, but his number was engaged. I'm going to ask him to come out here to see me as soon as he can . . . right away if possible—and I'm sure you would rather not be here when he arrives," she smiled gently.

He said that she was so right—David Sayer was not a man with whom he wished to become too friendly. The ex-Detective Chief Superintendent and his kind stood between him and his Destiny. Cyril Forbes had therefore vanished long before his sister had finished trying David Sayer's number again.

"Who was it?" David Sayer asked his wife when she returned to the kitchen after talking on the telephone for what had seemed to him an interminable length of time. "No, let me guess," he suggested, taking up the morning paper and frowning at the headlines. "Aunt Margaret! Well . . . who has the wicked madame clairvoyante tried to dispose of this time?"

"Lionel Preston," Jean Sayer replied, and in such an unusually flat tone of voice that her husband looked up sharply and gave her a long, hard look.

"Preston? What's happened to him?"

"Nobody seems to know. . . . Your aunt says that he vanished into thin air sometime yesterday afternoon. She said he went over to see Mrs Charles and never came back."

"How does she know he went to see Mrs Charles? Cissie Keith?"

"No—Cissie said he went out saying that he was going to walk over to the motorway . . . and he simply never came back. She got in touch with the police somewhere around eight last night and reported that he was missing, but they don't appear to have been too alarmed about it . . . not then, anyway. It's all a bit garbled—you know what your aunt is!—but the police apparently suggested to Cissie that he'd probably extended his walk and come over here, to Gidding. They seemed to think that when the weather worsened, he decided to stay the night here. . . ."

"He walked twenty-five miles in bad weather?" David Sayer sounded incredulous, understandably so.

"It would've been much less than that cross-country . . . half that distance. And that's what he appeared to be doing. A number of people saw him walking through the village, and then he was seen cutting across to the wood beyond Mrs Charles' bungalow. That's probably what made your aunt think that he was on his way to see Mrs Charles."

"Oh . . . so now we're getting down to it. She didn't actually see the dreadful spider lady lure him into her web and gobble him up alive?" He tut-tutted quietly. "I can remember being packed off to spend the occasional weekend with her when I was a youngster," he went on with a small, reflective smile. "She was living and working in London in those days, and you know, I couldn't understand why it was that there was something bad or wrong either about or with every single person who walked past her front window. Even as long ago as that she used to sit and watch everyone who went by and gossip about them." He pulled a face which was meant to resemble his aunt's and achieved an expression which made him look remarkably like her.

"Oooh, look, Davey . . ." he said mincingly. "There goes that dreadful Mrs XYZ. Look at that hat she's got on. What *does* she think she looks like? Who *does* she think she is?" He sighed and dropped the affected tone of *his* voice. "I was quite a big lad before I suddenly stopped watching the people outside her window and started taking one or two long hard looks at the person with me on my side." He seemed to give himself a little shake, as if shedding a particularly distasteful memory. Then, briskly, he continued:

"Anyway, what's the situation with Preston now? I hope he doesn't embarrass everybody by turning up in the wrong person's bedroom—if he is the ladies' man that Auntie would no doubt like to have us all think!"

"The police are searching the fields for him right now. They started at first light."

He stared at her for a moment. "So he didn't come over here, after all?"

"Apparently not."

"How did Auntie know that he was cutting across to the wood? I doubt if she could've seen that from her living-room window. . . ."

"Anne Blackmore saw him heading in that direction as she was on her way to visit Mrs Hatchard. Anne thought he looked as though he was going over to see Mrs Charles, and yet when she called round there a bit later on, he wasn't there. . . ."

"I wonder what Anne wanted with Mrs Charles?" he mused out loud.

"Your aunt said that she was returning Mrs Charles' shopping-basket—the one that Mrs Charles left with the strawberry jam the other day."

He shook his head wonderingly. "It's truly incredible. . . . Is there anything Aunt Margaret doesn't know?"

The telephone rang and Jean Sayer went into the hall to answer it. She returned a moment later, a curious expression on her face.

"It's spider lady," she hoarsely stage-whispered. "She wants to talk to you."

CHAPTER EIGHTEEN

Mrs Charles asked David Sayer to go on through to the sitting-room and to make himself comfortable while she fetched the tea-tray from the kitchen. She joined him a few moments later.

"The tea," she smiled, "should be nicely brewed: I made it when I heard you turn off the access road from the motorway."

"I must say you have exceptional hearing," he remarked.

"Yes—but I do have a little help. This bungalow is set in a hollow which seems to act as a sound-shell, particularly for any noise coming from the higher reaches of the access road. You came the other way round the last time you visited me . . . through the village," she smiled.

She poured the tea and offered him a plate of sweet biscuits. He took one and then looked up at her enquiringly.

"Have they found Mr Preston yet?" she asked, ignoring the question in his eyes. Then, before he could reply: "Cyril Forbes told me that there are policemen all over the village this morning, notably outside Mrs Keith's cottage and your aunt's place—though what possible connection Miss Sayer could have with Lionel Preston's disappearance has rather puzzled me . . . I confess that I've thought of little else ever since Cyril called round with the news."

"My wife spoke to her over the phone shortly before you rang. Aunt Margaret would appear to be a material witness to the man's disappearance. . . ."

"Miss Sayer does seem to lead the most extraordinarily active, exciting life," Mrs Charles murmured. "I don't think I could bear it myself—all that tension and suspense!"

"Aunt Margaret is one of two people who claim that Mr Preston was on his way to see you when he disappeared. Pure supposition, of course," he said offhandedly, as if it were an admission that he would rather not have had to make. "Both witnesses reached this conclusion following their close observation of the direction which Mr Preston took when setting out for a walk yesterday afternoon."

"May I ask the name of the second witness?"

"I understand that it was Anne Blackmore, the Vicar's wife."

Mrs Charles raised her eyebrows a little and sipped her tea. "Poor Cyril," she said after a moment. "I think he was rather hoping that he was the cause of all the police activity in the fields."

David Sayer frowned at her. "I thought you said it was Mr Forbes who told you what the police were doing in the village—?"

"—Or, in other words, Superintendent . . ." she smiled. "How do I know that Lionel Preston is missing? You told me . . . confirmed what I suspected. Lionel Preston's disappearance was—dare I say it?—predictable. He knew too much . . . but I don't think he realised it. I only spoke to him once, a very long time ago now, and he struck me then as being a feeble-minded sort of man, naïve . . . the kind of person who would unwittingly yet willingly allow himself to become involved in criminal complicacy. Subsequent events have confirmed that first impression I formed of him. It was a great pity he came here. I suppose one could say his luck finally ran out. He had the great misfortune not only to run into me and remember who I was, but to recall the terrible crime with which I had once been connected. The resultant gossip about me, so thoughtlessly fathered by him, sealed his fate."

"You speak as if Lionel Preston were dead," David Sayer observed.

"I shall be truly amazed if he is found otherwise," she said crisply. "Which does not augur well for me, does it, Superintendent?"

"I wouldn't think so, Mrs Charles," he said evenly. "Is he the reason for your wanting to see me?"

"No, he isn't. As a matter of fact, I had decided to call on you for help long before Cyril Forbes arrived this morning with the disquieting piece of news concerning the police."

"I cannot imagine anyone who needs help less than you do, Madame," he said coolly. "Especially my help."

"Ah, but there you are wrong, Superintendent." She smiled gravely at him. "I do need help, very specialized help . . . your help. Or are you no longer interested in seeing to it that Henrietta Player's murderer is brought to justice?"

Very deliberately David Sayer raised his cup to his lips and drank from it. With a gentle scrape, the cup was replaced in its saucer; then he looked up at Mrs Charles and said, "The last time I called on you, you made a point of assuring me that you were no hypocrite. Well, Mrs Charles, neither am I: therefore, even if I were in a position to give you the assistance that

you seek—the likelihood of which I very much
doubt—I would refuse on the grounds that I sincerely
believe that you, Madame, you and your half-brother,
Cyril Forbes, murdered Henrietta Player and, before
her, Janet Stuart. I am even predisposed to think that
you and your brother have also had a hand in Mr
Preston's disappearance."

Mrs Charles looked surprised. "But what else
would you think, Superintendent? Of course you believe me guilty of those crimes. That is why it is you,
aside from any other consideration, who must help me
to prove that I did no such thing as murder either
one of those poor, unfortunate women."

They stared at one another in silence. Then Mrs
Charles smiled gently and said, "I need a name, Superintendent—the last link in a terrible chain of
events. Without it I can prove nothing, neither my
innocence nor the guilt of the person who murdered
Janet Stuart and Henrietta Player. I did think of
sending Cyril back to get this name for me, but tomorrow is Wednesday and you know how he feels
about that particular day of the week. Besides, it
would take time, and if I'm right about Mr Preston,
time is the one advantage that I do not have. Mr
Preston is not the only one whose life is at some
risk. . . ."

"Perhaps now is a good moment for you to reflect
on the wisdom of your failing to take me into your
confidence when last I called to see you?" he suggested thinly.

"Pique does not suit you at all, Superintendent,"
she smiled. "You are far too big a man for such an
unbecoming attitude. Now . . . do we forget past
differences and join forces? Or is your masculine
pride so badly wounded that it has diminished your
respect for justice?"

He studied her for a very long moment without saying anything: then, finally—

"Very well, Mrs Charles: I won't promise that I can get you the name you want, but I'll try—provided that I can reserve the right to my male chauvinistic prejudice, none of which I yet see any just reason to revoke. . . ."

She nodded solemnly, but the blue eyes were smiling at him. "Is there some way that you can find out for me, quickly, the name of Janet Stuart's solicitor?"

He gave her a sharp look. "Surely that's something you already know?"

She shook her head. "Mrs Stuart never mentioned it to me—why should she? Neither was there ever any reference to the man by name in the newspapers at the time of her murder . . . at least not while I was still living in the town, although I do seem to recall someone—Mr Preston, I am inclined to think— telling me that the man whose name I now want wasn't a partner in the firm which represented her. He was, like Mr Preston, only an employee of this firm. As you probably already know, Superintendent, I left rather hurriedly . . . as soon as the police said that I was free to go . . . less than a week after the murder was committed. I was going through some rather unpleasant troubles of my own at that time—one of my husbands, of course: the second! He was threatening to expose the names of several of my clients—along with some privileged information which he claimed that he had acquired from me concerning them—to one of the less reputable newspapers. For a very large sum of money . . . which goes without saying," she put in dryly. "If I revealed the names of the persons concerned, you would understand the reason for my somewhat indecent haste to leave for London where my second husband was then living." She smiled again. "One way or another, my marriages have been most costly ventures, Superintendent . . . some people would even go so far as to say pathetic—" The smile faded and the expression in her eyes became oddly distant. "It never occurred to me before this moment, but I think that this will prove to be at the bottom of the Stuart murder . . . a pathetic marriage, one which should never have taken place."

She seemed almost visibly to shake herself out of her reverie, briskly continuing—

"This name I want . . . can you get it for me?"

"There is someone I could phone," he began slowly. "Detective Chief Superintendent Church. I think you may know him. . . ."

She smiled a little. "Yes. You remind me very much of him: he too had his little prejudices which he found difficult to contain. Poetic justice, wouldn't you say, that I am now proposing to make both of you my allies?"

He did not respond and seemed lost in thought.

"You are not at all sure that you won't be making a complete fool of yourself, are you, Superintendent?" she went on when the silence showed signs of lengthening interminably. "Get me that name and I promise you that I will tell you everything you want to know."

David Sayer went into the hall. As he began to talk on the telephone, Mrs Charles left the sofa for the chair which he had vacated. She had previously been sitting with her back to the door but was now facing it, and had David Sayer been less perplexed himself when he returned to the sitting-room some twelve minutes later, he would have observed that the expression in the eyes which watched his progress across the room conveyed something akin to his own extreme state of mental confusion.

He lowered himself on to the sofa, his eyes never leaving Mrs Charles' face. It was a very long time before either one of them spoke.

CHAPTER NINETEEN

The temporary closure of the Day Centre had left a great yawning gap in Miss Sayer's life. She had been glued to her living-room window for the best part of the morning with only the telephone and a short visit from Mrs Gee with the latest news on the situation at the Day Centre to break the monotony. She was thoroughly fed up, disgruntled with everything and everyone and the police in particular. It was inconceivable to her that anyone in his right mind would take the slightest bit of notice of something that Cissie Keith had said. . . .

Lionel Preston hadn't gone over to any motorway—and as for the police thinking that he might've walked on into Gidding and stayed there overnight when the weather turned bad . . . well, that was the dizzy limit! Lionel Preston was no better than David when it came to flexing his calf muscles: he never walked anywhere if he could possibly avoid it. Nearly knocked old Mrs Hatchard off her feet last Thursday in his rush to get himself and Cissie the best seats on the coach. Never mind that all the seats had been allocated in the proper democratic way, by drawing for them. He had no business to be on that coach, anyway. Miss Marsden was too soft. . . .

These were just a few of the thoughts concerning Lionel Preston which passed through Margaret

Sayer's head that morning, and very likely he would have continued so to occupy her mind had it not been for her nephew's visit to Mrs Charles.

Mrs Gee was responsible for this item of information which had been passed on to her by Colonel Billingsley with whom she had paused to chat in the High Street as she had been on her way to see Miss Sayer. Colonel Billingsley had contrived to take his early morning constitutional where it was bound to satisfy his curiosity about the activities of the police in the fields beyond Henrietta Player's cottage, and while he had been walking back to the village, David Sayer had driven past him—on his way, Colonel Billingsley had carefully noted a short while later, to see Mrs Charles.

With the front gate barely closed behind Mrs Gee, Miss Sayer had changed her house shoes for a pair of sturdy, fur-lined boots which were more suited to the wet day, and put on her almost-new brown, gold and white check coat. Hastily she tied a clear, pleated plastic hood over the snug-fitting felt hat which she had pressed down hard round her ears; then she grabbed up an umbrella and went out. Her blood pressure was rising rapidly. The muscles of her arms, hands and stomach quivered with nervous tension.

Betty and Dorothy, two of Mr Roper's Friesians, spared her a long thoughtful look as she passed the dairy, but she was far too preoccupied to notice their interest in her.

Abruptly she left the footpath and plunged through a gap in the hedgerow and started across an open field towards the small wood which ran along the bottom of Mrs Charles' garden. In the distance, on Miss Sayer's left, were half a dozen police officers with sticks and two dogs; but if their speed of movement—general lack of purpose, Miss Sayer observed sourly to herself—were anything for her to go by, she would arrive at the wood days before they did. . . . If they had listened to her and taken a little less notice of Mrs Glamour-puss Blackmore and that soppy Cissie Keith they would've found Lionel Preston hours ago.

Nearing the wood, she saw that Colonel Billingsley had been right about her nephew. His car was parked on Mrs Charles' drive. Miss Sayer's mouth tightened resentfully. Jean hadn't said anything to her on the phone about David coming over to the village to-day—and she would bet a pound to a penny that he would turn right round and go back to the motorway without it once entering his head that it would be nice to drive on into the village and say hello to her.

She turned away and marched resolutely into the misty, dank-smelling wood, taking the narrow foot-path which she knew would bring her out near Henrietta Player's cottage. . . . At which precise moment, Mrs Charles was opening a black jewel-case and holding it out to Margaret Sayer's nephew so that he could inspect its contents at close quarters.

An exquisite gold necklace, magnificently set with more diamonds than David Sayer had seen in any one piece of jewellery since a childhood visit to see the Crown-jewels in the Tower of London, was laid out on a black velvet base. His low whistle expressed his sentiments without the need for words.

"I meant it very sincerely when I told you the other day that I always felt that while I kept this necklace, there was every possibility that I would discover the identity of Janet Stuart's murderer . . . that he or she would eventually have to come after it; and I was right," Mrs Charles said. "I was followed here to the village, or rather Cyril was, Janet Stuart's murderer knowing full well that in time I was bound to join him. . . ."

"I wonder how much it was her and not him?" David Sayer mused out loud. "Did he push her into it?"

They were both very quiet for a moment or two: then he frowned across at Mrs Charles and said:

"The evidence against her is so circumstantial . . . too circumstantial. I don't see that it would be any use going to the police with what you've told me. Perhaps—and it's a big perhaps—they'd dig out the Stuart and the Player murder cases and give them both another airing in the light of this fresh evidence, but personally I doubt it: I can't help feeling that their view would be the same as mine, and that in the long run they would find themselves stuck hard and fast in the mud with the same conclusion. There's nowhere near enough evidence for an arrest and a conviction . . . a foregone conclusion and an expensive one in terms of wasted manpower: that's how they'll look at it . . . and nobody's going to thank either one of us for making nuisances of ourselves. You could even find yourself in some pretty hot water, too . . . for withholding information—particularly about the painting that you now say was missing from Miss Player's sitting-room. Some might even think your story about the chap Mr Forbes brought here last night a little too convenient for yourself," he pointed out, raising his eyebrows at her.

She nodded her agreement: then, after a moment, she looked down at the necklace and studied it thoughtfully.

"She wanted this very badly once, Superintendent," she said at length. "Badly enough that first she almost drove a poor, defenceless old lady out of her mind and then finally, losing patience, she callously murdered her for it. I think we are both agreed that she followed Cyril here in the hope that one day an opportunity would present itself whereby she would find herself in a position to wrest it from me. A small thing like time, having to wait that little bit longer to get what one wants, wouldn't dull the edge of desire of such a person. . . ."

She raised her eyes to his. "I understand that the church steeple was badly damaged in that severe electric storm we had last summer. . . . I often wondered why the Blackmores approached neither Cyril nor myself directly for a contribution to the fund for its replacement: one should support one's community, if not in the giving of some of one's time, then by financial contribution. I have perhaps been a little remiss in this area in the past, Superintendent—"

He gave her a very long, hard look. "You're not thinking of donating the Stuart necklace to St Stephen's building fund?" he asked, astonished.

"I am very partial to diamonds," she smiled, "but only in rings, and it would be unthinkable to have this exquisite setting broken down in any way; so there will be no conflict of desires."

They stared at one another for quite some time, neither speaking. Then David Sayer narrowed his eyes and said, "Am I right—? Are you suggesting that prior to its sale, the Stuart necklace should be put on display somewhere in the village?"

An outer door was flung open with a loud bang. Seconds later, a demented, panting figure burst in upon them.

Glassy-eyed, Margaret Sayer stood swaying in the doorway. She was hatless, the tight while curls covering her head glistening with droplets of moisture, while the plastic rain-hood hung uselessly round her neck like a baby's bib. There was a button missing from her coat, which was more off than on, and her boots were thick with mud which was also splattered over her stockinged legs and the lower part of both her pleated woolen skirt and her coat.

For a very long moment she stared hypnotically at the necklace in Mrs Charles' hand. Then her face and mouth began to work furiously.

"*Murderer!*" she finally cried out hoarsely. She staggered forward, falling in a dead faint at Mrs Charles' feet.

CHAPTER TWENTY

The villagers were shocked. The murder of Henrietta Player had been bad enough, but this—it was monstrous and it chilled the blood to think of it. *"Decapitated!"* Miss Sayer said, though this was later denied by Cissie Keith, whose unfortunate lot it had been to make the formal identification of her cousin's body.

The police, Cissie Keith told everyone, were of the opinion that Lionel had been down on all fours searching for his spectacles. . . . No, she couldn't say what the spectacles were doing on the ground and why Lionel wasn't wearing them, but there was a handkerchief bearing his initials found near his body which had led the police to suspect that he could have been cleaning the lenses in his spectacles when he heard something or someone coming up behind him which startled him, causing him to drop them.

Cissie Keith then went on to say that while Lionel was groping about, trying to find them, he was struck low on the back of the neck with an axe which the police know for sure belongs to Cyril Forbes. Cyril Forbes had used the axe at the beginning of winter to chop up some firewood for Mrs Charles and had left it there in the wood when he had finished. Cissie Keith was told that her cousin had died instantly. The blade of the axe had severed his spinal cord.

It was widely accepted in the village that poor mad Cyril Forbes would be charged with the murder of Cissie Keith's cousin. The popular theory (one to which Margaret Sayer steadfastly refused to subscribe) was that while he had been out walking on Monday afternoon, Lionel Preston had accidentally stumbled across Cyril Forbes' motorway secret, and that the madness which all were agreed that Cyril Forbes had suffered from for years had finally become a murderous insanity.

The thin line of Miss Sayer's lips got straighter and harder as one by one her friends from the Day Centre dropped by to see her and contributed their little bit to the mountain of evidence against Cyril Forbes. Miss Sayer was being kept mildly sedated and was confined to bed under the watchful eye of her nephew and his wife, who had moved into one of the spare bedrooms of her cottage until she was back on her feet again.

Ninety-year-old Eve Hatchard visited her on Friday morning, three days after Miss Sayer had made her ghastly discovery in the wood, her graphic account of which was prematurely brought to a close by the kind of inanity that, in Miss Sayer's own words, 'Made her blood boil'!

"It wasn't Mr Forbes who did it," Mrs Hatchard announced in the firm, clear voice which belied her years. "He was in London—or rather, was on his way back from London when Cissie's cousin was murdered. I heard that Mr Forbes still had his ticket stubs when the police went to see him about that axe of his, and at least two people from Gidding have come forward and said that he got off the late Monday afternoon train from Waterloo with them."

"You're not telling me anything that I don't already know and haven't been trying to get through everyone's thick skull these past two or three days!" Miss Sayer snapped. She was feeling much better and spoke to the other woman as if she were twenty years her junior and not the reverse. "The police are as thickheaded as the rest of you. That woman did it— that Mrs Charles!"

"Oh, no, you're wrong there, Miss Sayer." Mrs Hatchard shook her head and looked very definite about it. "Mrs Charles couldn't have murdered Lionel Preston. Mrs Blackmore said so. . . . She was with Mrs Charles when he died."

"I don't believe it," Miss Sayer said firmly. "And if the police have any sense, which I doubt, they won't either! You mark my words, there's been a mistake somewhere, a terrible mistake . . . one after the other," she muttered, almost in an aside. "It's as plain as the nose on your face—that man tried to warn us . . . he was a threat to her, so first she tried to poison him and then, when that failed, she tricked him into meeting her alone in the wood, where she axed him to death. Just you wait and see if I'm not right. . . ."

"I don't know," the other woman said hesitantly. "I think you could be mistaken there. . . . You're definitely wrong about the food poisoning that made us ill. Nobody's having too much to say about it now . . . certainly no one down at the Day Centre, but you know yourself that the Department of Health has ordered that the kitchen must be spruced up a bit, and several people have told me that Mrs Gee has had a terrible dressing-down from one of the health inspectors and Miss Marsden because she handled food all last week with a sore finger. The dressing she had over it, which I was told was very soiled and hadn't been changed since she'd first cut her finger, could've contaminated any food that she handled."

For a fleeting instant, Miss Sayer looked doubtful. Then she recovered herself. "We didn't have a meal at the Day Centre the day we all took sick . . . and it's nonsense to suggest that it was the shepherd's pie we had on the Wednesday—it took too long to affect us."

"I'm not so sure about that, Miss Sayer," Mrs Hatchard said. "Sometimes food poisoning can react very quickly, within a matter of a few hours of the consumption of any contaminated food; and in other cases, it can take much longer to have any effect—a day or more, I once read somewhere. Anyway, if it was the shepherd's pie from the previous day, it would explain why Lionel Preston wasn't ill. He wasn't allowed to have any meals at the Day Centre, but Cissie—if you remember—came down specially that Wednesday . . . the day we had shepherd's pie . . . to check on the arrangements for the coach outing, and she was sick. So was Mrs Blackmore, and she had lunch with us that day, too . . . sat at our table! I'll be very surprised if we ever get a satisfactory answer from anybody about it: the health people probably know what caused the sickness, but we'll never be told what their official findings were, especially if all was not as it should've been in the Day Centre's kitchen. The local authority wouldn't be too anxious to invite any criticism of the standard of service that they've been providing for their senior citizens."

Miss Sayer thought for a moment. Then, always the one with the last word on everything, she said:

"I hope that dirty cat Joyce Gee was also told about that filthy smoking habit of hers . . . always

puffing her smoke over everything and everyone
. . . it's disgusting! Everything is so slap-dash these
days. Whatever's happened to the good old-fashioned
standards that were so important to everyone when
we were young? Some of the things that I've seen
happen this last week or so . . . people's attitudes—I don't honestly think that anything I heard or
saw would surprise me any more!"

Miss Sayer was put severely to the test that evening
when her nephew's wife broke the news to her about
the Stuart necklace—

"Mrs Charles is giving it to the church," Jean Sayer
informed her. "It's to be sold, of course, but the en-
tire proceeds of sale will go into St Stephen's building
fund."

"Frank Blackmore won't accept a penny of it!"
Miss Sayer said emphatically. "He's got too much in-
tegrity. There's blood on those diamonds."

"I understand that Frank has already written a letter to Mrs Charles on behalf of himself and the
church-wardens formally thanking her for the gift."

"I refuse to believe it!" Miss Sayer retorted.

"It's perfectly true—I met Anne in the High Street
today and she told me so herself. She's very excited
about it."

"She would be," Miss Sayer said tartly. "Little
madam! Well, you listen to me, my girl: no good will
come of it. I've never seen anything so wicked-looking
as those stones in that necklace . . . my blood ran
cold when I saw that evil woman sitting there with it
in her hand, gloating over it."

"The necklace can't mean that much to her if she's
prepared to part with it as readily as David says she
is."

"The woman's damned, and she knows it. She's

using that necklace to buy her salvation . . . that's what she's up to, my girl!"

Margaret Sayer's dark eyes were fired with a wild, unreasoning passion which made her nephew's wife feel that she was looking at her not as she was now but as she could be in a few years' time. Insanity? Jean wondered with a shudder. Was that what lay ahead of the old lady if these unreasonable prejudices, this bitterness, were allowed to continue unchecked?

"You don't like Mrs Charles one little bit, do you?" the younger woman remarked thoughtfully.

"That should be obvious. She's worse than the new-comers! They might be a pain in the neck, the way they want to change and rearrange the village into the neat, nondescript middle-class suburbia that they've always known, but at least they're making some, albeit misguided, attempt to become one of us. Mrs Charles and that idiot brother of hers have always gone their own way, never given a damn about any of us!"

"I wouldn't say that. Cyril Forbes cared passionately about the motorway . . . and there were a lot of people who felt the same way he did about its present location and wanted it where he suggested it should be . . . even David felt there was a strong agrument for it!"

"Next you'll be telling me that David plans to join him in his madness every Wednesday afternoon."

"Cyril Forbes isn't the only one around here who claims to have spotted U.F.O.s," Jean Sayer said defensively. "There was that strange ball of fire that Mr Roper photographed a few years back—you can't say that that was imagination. It gave some of his cows such a fright that their milk dried up."

"That woman and her brother have bewitched the lot of you!" Miss Sayer exclaimed in amazement. "You'll all be sitting out there in the fields drinking tea and waiting for . . . what does that fool call it? *The Coming!* Well, you won't catch me listening to any of that rubbish and gushing over Mrs Charles and her necklace."

Jean Sayer contrived an innocent expression. "You mean you won't be going down to the Day Centre to have a look at it on Monday?"

Miss Sayer gave her an odd look.

"You don't know—?" The younger woman smiled to herself. "Oh . . . I thought Mrs Hatchard would've told you while she was here this afternoon, but she obviously hasn't heard about it herself yet. The Blackmores have got permission to use the television room on Monday afternoon so that everyone can have a look at the necklace before it's taken to London to be sold."

"It's morbid—you know that, don't you? Nothing but horrid, morbid curiosity!" Miss Sayer said vehemently. "You should all be ashamed of yourselves. Have you no thought, no feeling at all for the poor murdered woman who owned that necklace?"

Jean Sayer tossed her head carelessly. "Well, I'm going down to see it . . . you can please yourself what you do! Some of the ladies are putting on afternoon tea—I thought it would make a very nice little outing for the three of us . . . David wants to have another look at it, so we could all go together."

Miss Sayer snorted. Then she eyed Jean curiously and asked, "Who's taking the necklace to London?"

"Mrs Charles is. What do any of us know about diamonds and what they're worth?"

"Hah!" said Miss Sayer. "I thought so. Well, my

girl, you can take my word for it that that'll be the last any of you will see of those diamonds and Madame Adele Herrmann alias Mrs Edwina Charles!"

CHAPTER TWENTY-ONE

Miss Marsden and her helpers at the Day Centre went to a lot of bother. Colonel Billingsley's late brother had collected butterflies during his lifetime and one of his display-cases, which were still in Colonel Billingsley's possession, was borrowed for the day and centred on a green, baize-covered trestle-table. Someone else had provided the black velvet on which, shortly after two thirty on the following Monday afternoon, Mrs Charles carefully laid the Stuart necklace.

The centre of the large room where the members of the Day Centre could take their early morning coffee if they wished had been cleared. Small tables and chairs had been arranged across the back of the room and along one wall. The long trestle-table on which Miss Marsden's helpers had set up the tea urn and laid out the crockery for afternoon tea was along another wall. The Stuart necklace in its butterfly display-case had been placed near the wall where the television set usually stood.

Miss Marsden unlocked the doors of the Day Centre at three, warmly greeting the large gathering waiting patiently outside in thin, wintry sunshine. To avoid any jostling of the very old and those with physical disabilities (and any bad feeling!), the members of the Day Centre were given priority over every-

one else and were first to file with meek expectancy
into the television room and then pass slowly in front
of the display-case. Margaret Sayer, Cissie Keith and
Florrie Fenton were the last of the over sixty-fives to
enter the room, having been reluctantly compelled to
contain their child-like impatience to see the infa-
mous piece of jewellery because the wife of Mrs
Sayer's nephew was with them.

Neither Miss Sayer nor her nephew and his wife,
who had decided to stay on in the village until after
the public showing of the Stuart necklace, had made
any further reference to Miss Sayer's declaration of
indifference about the whole affair—which seemed to
have completely slipped her mind. Over breakfast
that morning she had outlined her activities for the
day, all of which had been notably influenced by her
proposed three o'clock visit to the Day Centre to see
the Stuart necklace.

Jean Sayer looked across at her husband and
winked as she entered the room. He was standing
with Mrs Charles and the Blackmores to one side of
the table from which Miss Marsden and several other
ladies were busily dispensing hot tea and biscuits to
those who had seen the necklace.

Miss Sayer flicked a disapproving eye over the display-case and its contents and a moment later was dis-
tinctly heard to mutter 'Silly cat!' when Cissie Keith
predictably issued forth with what appeared to be the
requisite 'ooh aahs!'

Jean Sayer paused to speak to her husband and
Mrs Charles, but Miss Sayer pressed resolutely on,
calling irritably to Mrs Keith and Mrs Fenton—both
of whom had shown an inclination to want to stop
and talk to Miss Sayer's nephew and Mrs Charles—
that there would be no tea left if they didn't hurry
up.

David Sayer turned to his wife and said:

"I think I should run Mrs Charles home after this is all over—I don't like the idea of her walking home alone in the dark with the necklace on her."

Miss Sayer handed Mrs Keith her tea and then glowered round her at David. *That woman had him eating out of the palm of her hand!*

Mrs Charles said, "No, Superintendent: thank you all the same, but that won't be necessary. Cyril promised that he would come and collect me. He's having dinner with me this evening so that we can finalise the arrangements for the trip up to London later this week: he has decided to accompany me."

Although taking no part herself in the conversation between her nephew and Mrs Charles, Miss Sayer nodded her satisfaction with Mrs Charles' arrangements for getting home: then Miss Sayer, the other two women and Mrs Gee, who had since joined them, moved on to find a vacant chair for Mrs Fenton who was complaining loudly about the varicose veins in her right leg.

By four thirty, an estimated two hundred and fifty people, mostly women (few of whom were more interested in the Stuart necklace than in its donor), had filed past the display-case and approximately one hundred and fifty cups of tea had been consumed. Most people had gone home. Margaret Sayer was one of the few who had remained behind, but in her case it was not from choice. She was waiting with increasing ill-will for Cissie Keith who had been helping to clear away the afternoon tea things.

After several false starts ("Cissie Keith," Miss Sayer grumbled to Anne Blackmore, "would forget her head if it wasn't for the fact that it's securely stitched on!"), Miss Sayer and Mrs Keith finally left, barely a minute ahead of the Blackmores and David and Jean Sayer.

In the manner of the two women who had preceded them out of the Day Centre, the Blackmores and the Sayers walked together as far as The Brewery and there parted company.

"Well," Jean Sayer sighed once she and her husband were alone, "that was a let down. Nothing happened—!"

David seemed mildly astonished. "With all those people about? What did you expect?"

"I don't really know," she admitted thoughtfully. "I was watching her closely and I'm positive that she heard you and Mrs Charles discussing how she would get home—and I wonder if she'll follow Mrs Charles and Mr Forbes and try to get the necklace when Mrs Charles is on her own?" She paused, then frowning: "She'll have to move quickly . . . that is if she believed what Mrs Charles said about taking the necklace to London before the end of the week."

"I'm pretty sure she's already made her move—didn't you notice that there was no one in sight by the time we reached The Brewery?"

Jean shrugged a little. "No . . . I was too busy saying goodbye to Anne and Frank. Anyway, I can't see that it's so very significant that there was no one about: you know what your aunt is like when she's incensed about something . . . and she was really fizzing back there over Cissie and her dawdling—she moves like a rocket when she's angry about something."

David was shaking his head. "My guess is that she ducked into the loading bay round the other side of The Brewery and waited there until she saw the Blackmores and ourselves go our separate ways."

Jean looked alarmed. "You mean she's gone back to the Day Centre?"

They paused as they reached the front gate to Margaret Sayer's cottage and Jean looked round nervously. "Shouldn't you go back and make sure that Mrs Charles is all right?" she asked.

He gazed down the road at The Brewery and something like regret showed in his eyes.

"Nothing will happen to her there." His voice carried conviction, but his face was shaded with doubt. He couldn't quite make himself believe that he could ever feel that sure about something over which he had absolutely no control. "Cyril Forbes," he went on, "will probably be there now, anyway."

"He can't be . . . not yet. We would've seen him go by."

"If he's on his bike, he might've gone round the other way."

Jean shivered a little. "I'd sooner it was her life dependent on him than mine," she remarked as they went inside.

Miss Marsden said, "I hate to rush off and leave you like this, Mrs Charles. You're sure you'll be all right here on your own?"

Mrs Charles assured her that she would. "My brother should be along any moment now," she added.

Miss Marsden slipped on her coat, a very smart camel-hair with a fox-fur trim, and gathered up her things. "The door locks automatically," she said. "Just pull it to when you go." She knotted the tie on her coat and held out her hand. "I'll say good-night then, Mrs Charles. It's been a most interesting afternoon," she smiled. "I wouldn't have missed it for anything!"

Miss Marsden went out, leaving one side of the main doors a little ajar for Cyril Forbes. Mrs Charles, who had gone as far as the passage with Miss Marsden, turned back into the television room, paused to switch on the light and then sat down in a big, comfortable arm-chair. The room had been returned to its normal arrangement of half a dozen or so arm-chairs and a number of small tables and chairs positioned in a semi-circle before the television set.

Several minutes later, she heard someone in the outer passage. She knew not to expect that it would be her brother. His movements were always the same, no matter what the circumstances or surroundings in which he found himself—quick, nervous darting . . . very much like those of a small bird. The footsteps to which Mrs Charles were listening were slow, unsure, hesitant.

CHAPTER TWENTY-TWO

Mrs Charles folded her hands in her lap and waited. She couldn't see into the passage: the door was half-closed.

The footsteps reached the doorway and stopped. It was very quiet. The moments lengthened into a minute, and then the door swung silently open.

"Oh!" Cissie Keith exclaimed. "You're still waiting for Mr Forbes, Mrs Charles. I thought everyone had gone home and forgotten to lock the front door . . . it was open." She looked vaguely about her. "I've left my gloves behind—you haven't seen them anywhere, have you? Miss Sayer was in such a rush to get away that I didn't get a proper chance to collect all of my things together. She makes me so nervous," she complained with a frown. "Gets me so that I don't know whether I'm coming or going. . . ." She glanced round the room. "I must've left them in the kitchen. I probably put them down somewhere out there when I went to give a hand with the clearing up."

She went to go on through to the kitchen, but Mrs Charles stopped her.

"You really must visit me one afternoon, Mrs Keith . . . allow me to read the Tarot for you, or perhaps gaze in the crystal . . . it could be of great benefit to you, particularly if, as you say, you are inclined to be of a nervous disposition. Perhaps Miss Sayer would like to accompany you—?"

"Ooh, I don't think so," Mrs. Keith said quickly. "Miss Sayer doesn't have any time for that sort of thing."

Mrs Charles smiled a little. "I suspect that it would be more to the point to say that Miss Sayer has no time for me."

Cissie Keith looked uncomfortable. "Miss Sayer doesn't like anyone very much."

There was a moment's silence. Then Mrs Charles smiled gravely and said, "Does she really think I'm going to vanish overnight and that that'll be the last any of you will ever see of me and the necklace?"

"How—?" Cissie Keith didn't finish. She frowned and nervously chewed a corner of her mouth: then, after a slight hesitation, she asked, curiously, "Is it true?"

Mrs Charles laughed lightly. "No, of course it isn't true. The necklace has served its purpose, finally laid Janet Stuart's ghost to rest. I can now, in all good conscience, allow it to pass from my possession. I have no further use for it."

She went to her handbag and removed the jewel-case which contained the necklace. She opened it up and started to laugh. "Paste, Mrs Keith—and nobody was any the wiser," she said, holding out the jewel-case to the other woman. "What do you think the necklace will fetch? Fifty pounds?"

Cissie Keith's face went slack. Saliva collected in the corners of her drooping mouth. "You sold it," she whispered hoarsely. *"You sold the Stuart necklace!"*

"Of course I did. Years ago."

"But—" Cissie Keith's almost colourless eyes looked as though they had slipped out of focus. Then, after a moment, her gaze sharpened and she continued:

"We're two of a kind, you and I—we couldn't sell them . . . not those diamonds. We'd do anything to keep them . . . even kill."

"No, Mrs Keith," Mrs Charles said quietly. "You're wrong there. I wouldn't kill for the Stuart diamonds, but you would—you've already killed once for that necklace, haven't you?"

The washed-out eyes slipped momentarily out of focus again. "She wouldn't give it to me—everything else but that necklace; and then she was going to make a will . . ."

"Did your husband know that you had been threatening Janet Stuart?"

Cissie Keith tossed back her head. She was in the centre of the room, standing directly beneath the naked light bulb, the harsh glare from which played bizarre tricks with her orange hair. "It would've been so easy. If only he'd listened to me. There were so many of them: rich, whining old women. Selfish, they were: all of them . . . had him running round in circles looking after them and their affairs, day and night . . . never gave him a moment's peace. No thanks he ever got from anyone. Those people he worked for just took it all for granted . . . never a word about taking him into partnership. Don't you see what a wonderful opportunity it was for us? 'Janet Stuart is only the beginning,' I said to him. But no, he wouldn't listen to me: not my Desmond. When he found out about me and Janet Stuart, he gave up his job and retired. It was either that, he said, or he would have to have me committed in case it happened again. '*Committed*,' he said . . . just like that! *As if I was mad!*" She stared distractedly at Mrs Charles, and again as Mrs Charles watched her, her gaze appeared to slip temporarily out of focus—a clear indication, Mrs Charles felt, of how perilously close Cissie Keith was to toppling over the edge into total insanity.

Mrs Charles kept her voice quiet and calm. "But your husband let you choose your place of retirement—?"

The look of sly cunning in Cissie Keith's eye revealed in full the reverse side of her personality. The weak, vapid creature who trailed in Margaret Sayer's wake in a nervous confusion of lost articles and indecision was, Mrs Charles realised, nothing but a clever masquerade for the real person, the real Cissie Keith, whom she was now seeing for the first time.

"I was very clever, wasn't I?" It was a trick of the light and possibly, Mrs Charles suspected, of her own imagination, but Cissie Keith's face looked as though it was becoming fat and bloated with gloating. "My Desmond never suspected a thing," Cissie Keith went on, "not even afterwards . . . after he found out that Cyril Forbes was living here. He had no idea that I was really waiting for you. And I knew that you'd turn up sooner or later. I just had to be patient. I'd get my diamonds one day. . . ."

"And in the meanwhile your husband passed on and you heard all the stories about the money which Henrietta Player was said to keep hidden under the flooring-boards of her cottage. The temptation was too great, wasn't it?"

Cissie Keith eyed her defiantly. "She would've given it all away in the finish, anyway—to all those people she used to let sponge off her."

"So you did find some money in her cottage?"

"No," Cissie Keith said crossly. "She wasted my time. It was all talk. She had nothing. *Nothing!* A few ugly old pictures . . . everything else had gone years ago. I could've killed her!" she finished vehemently.

"But, Mrs Keith . . . you *did* kill her." Mrs Charles said gravely, "You haven't forgotten, have you?"

Cissie Keith looked momentarily confused. Then she frowned and said, "Oh, yes, I remember now. . . . She was such a silly, stubborn woman. She was like that Janet Stuart I used to know a long time ago. She made me very angry. I don't like people who make me angry."

"Did your cousin Lionel make you angry, too?"

The madness in Cissie Keith's brain briefly illuminated her eyes. There was a sickening grin on her lips. "All those years . . ." she gloated. "He never once suspected . . . always did everything I told him to do with never a question. His own fault. I told him he was naïve. Then Mrs Blackmore came round to see me the other day and it happened . . . after all that time, *Lionel knew—*"

"How did he know, Mrs Keith?" Mrs Charles asked quietly. "You must have said or done something after all those years to make him suspect that it was you and not I who had murdered Janet Stuart—"

"Oh, yes, of course . . ." the other woman said, a disturbingly vacant expression on her face. "It was when I told Mrs Blackmore that my Desmond and I came here eight years ago, a year or so after Margaret Sayer returned to the village to live. I could see Lionel subtracting the years . . . working it all out in his head. You see, a day or two earlier I had let it slip that Mr Forbes had come here in nineteen sixty-six, which meant that he was here first, not us. . . ."

"You'd let your cousin think that you and your husband were the first to move to the village and that it was by sheer coincidence that my brother and I should also choose to settle here?"

The other woman did not reply, but her sickly grin flickered a little.

"Did your cousin make any reference to it . . . to this slip you made about when you came here to live?" Mrs Charles asked after a moment.

Cissie Keith narrowed her eyes. "He went over to see Mr Forbes. I followed him—I was very clever about it, too . . . like I was when I used to go over to see Henrietta Player. I knew Margaret Sayer would be sitting there in that window of hers watching Lionel, even though it was late and getting dark, so I went round the other way and nobody, not a living soul, saw me." Her face shone with child-like glee, and then, almost as if a shadow had suddenly fallen across her, her expression darkened. "I caught up with him in the wood at the bottom of your garden."

She paused and frowned at Mrs Charles. "I thought Lionel was on his way to see you, but that wasn't what he planned at all. I watched and waited, and then he went on, and I knew what he was going to do . . . he was going behind my back to talk to that silly Mr Forbes about me and my Desmond and Janet Stuart and all the rest of it; and that made me angry. *Very* angry. He promised my Desmond and he promised me *faithfully*—only the other day, too—that he would never tell anybody that my Desmond was Janet Stuart's solicitor. That was what he was going to tell Mr Forbes, and it was supposed to be a secret between just the three of us . . . my Desmond and Lionel and me. People *will* talk, you know," she said earnestly. "I told Lionel we didn't want any gossip about us, but he took no notice of me. I was very cross with him."

"So you waited in the wood until he came back and then you killed him with my brother's axe, the one you'd found lying about there somewhere?" Mrs Charles said quietly.

"It was easy," Cissie Keith said with a derisive laugh. "Not like it was with that Janet Stuart and Henrietta Player." She drew her eyebrows together in a tight, angry frown. "I told them to be still, but they wouldn't listen. I get very angry when people won't listen to me."

Mrs Charles studied her for a moment; then she quietly closed the lid of the jewel-case and said, very softly, "What a shame. . . . All the trouble you went to for nothing but a cheap, paste necklace."

Cissie Keith's right hand was inside the large, white plastic shopper which she was carrying over her left arm. When she withdrew her hand, it was clasping the long carving knife which she had stolen from the kitchen-dresser a short while earlier while helping Mrs Gee and Mrs Fenton with the washing-up. She took a step towards Mrs Charles. "It was all your fault," she said accusingly, anger showing in the whites of her eyes which had suddenly become luminously bright. "Janet Stuart would've given me the necklace if it hadn't been for your interference. You gave her the courage to stand up to me. I had to kill her, you understand. She made me angry. . . ." She raised her arm.

"Come now, Mrs Keith. . . ."

The voice, Detective Chief Superintendent Fred Church's, came from the doorway of the short connecting passage between the kitchen and the television room. He went on:

"What would Miss Marsden say if you made her nice clean floor all messy? I don't think she'd be at all pleased—"

Shock momentarily froze Cissie Keith to the spot. And then she started to laugh shrilly. It was a terrible sound which filled the room and became increasingly louder and unrestrained. No resistance was put up when the knife was taken from her and handed to the plain-clothes man who had followed up behind the Superintendent. Two uniformed police constables quickly brought up the rear and, with one on either side of her, Mrs Keith was led screeching from the room.

Superintendent Church, a heavily-built, red-faced man in his early fifties, turned to Mrs Charles and said, "It's been a long time, Madame. Ten years, I believe. You are looking very well."

She smiled at the compliment. "I confess to feeling considerably better than I was a little while ago when it suddenly occurred to me that something might've gone wrong with Superintendent Sayer's plan and I could very well be here all on my own with Mrs Keith."

Superintendent Church took the jewel-case from her and had a long look at the necklace.

"Did you really sell the real one?" he asked her curiously.

She smiled gravely at him and retrieved the jewel-case, placing it in her handbag which was then snapped shut on an unmistakable note of finality. "That, Superintendent, is going to be my little secret."

CHAPTER TWENTY-THREE

"When did you first suspect Cissie Keith?" Jean Sayer asked.

David and Jean Sayer had returned to Gidding on Monday evening, but at the invitation of Mrs Charles had driven over to the village again on the following Wednesday afternoon. Mrs Charles had specially baked a chocolate fudge cake for afternoon tea, the receipe for which she said was her own, with one of her grave smiles adding that all three of her ex-husbands had been extremely partial to it. She was cutting David Sayer a generous slice of the cake as Jean put her question to her.

"The day I ran into her and her cousin in the village," Mrs Charles replied. "I was suddenly overcome by the most extraordinary feeling that I had seen her somewhere before, somewhere other than around here."

"That wasn't the first time that you'd run into her in the village, surely?" Jean said, a little surprised and disappointed that Mrs Charles' disclosure had not been of a more dramatic nature.

"No, of course not, my dear. It was seeing her with Lionel Preston that made that meeting so very different from all the other times I had seen her."

David Sayer paused between mouthfuls of Mrs Charles' chocolate fudge cake, which was truly delicious, to say, " '*Shook rigid*' was the expression my aunt used to describe the effect Cissie's cousin had on you that day."

"Ah, yes," Mrs Charles said thoughtfully, and smiled. "A fair description, I would say, of one's reaction to having been transported back ten years in a split second to a particularly unpleasant and tragic episode of one's life. I recognised Lionel Preston instantly—he had altered so little over the years: bachelors seldom do change much," she smiled. "He came to my home shortly after Mrs Stuart was murdered: he'd been sent to see me by the executor of her will, who also happened to be her solicitor—"

"Desmond Keith, Cissie's husband," Jean Sayer said.

"Yes," Mrs Charles nodded. "Although at that time I was completely ignorant of the man's name. Newspaper references to Mrs Stuart's legal representative gave only the name of the firm which employed Mr Keith."

"Trembath, Lewisham and Partners," David Sayer interjected. "Desmond Keith was never taken into partnership—for a number of reasons, Fred Church has since found out . . . one of them Mrs Keith. They never felt that Cissie and one or two members of her family quite came up to the corporate image. A stuffy lot, by all accounts: even today. . . . Though, with hindsight, one can now say it was probably the wisest decision they ever made."

Mrs Charles nodded and went on:

"Mr Preston asked me if I would be prepared to return Mrs Stuart's necklace to her estate—an elderly sister-in-law of Mrs Stuart's, who lived in America, was her sole beneficiary . . . I understand from Superintendent Church that she died shortly before probate of Mrs Stuart's will was granted. But that is by the by. . . . When Lionel Preston came to see me, the beneficiary was very much alive and particularly anxious to have the necklace, so anxious in fact that Mr Preston said that he was authorised by the executor of Mrs Stuart's will to offer me a certain sum of money if I would agree to hand it over. I refused. Not because I wanted the necklace for myself or indeed believed that I had any right to keep it. I declined simply because I knew that if I allowed it to leave my possession to be sent to America, Mrs Stuart's murderer would never be found. It was all there in the crystal, the vision of myself in an atmosphere of great danger—"

"David told me that when you gazed in the crystal for Mrs Stuart on the night she died, you saw yourself wearing the Stuart necklace and yet you knew nothing about it," Jean Sayer interrupted with a frown.

Mrs Charles smiled to herself at the doubt in Jean's voice, but she made no attempt to expound upon her clairvoyance. One either believed, *wanted* to believe, or one didn't: it was a decision which she always allowed people to make for themselves.

"That is quite so, my dear," she agreed. "I had never seen the Stuart necklace before that night, and Mrs Stuart had certainly never made any reference to it . . . to any of her possessions, for that matter. I knew next to nothing about her. However, two days later—Mrs Stuart had come to see me on the Saturday night, the night she was murdered, and this was now the following Monday morning—I received a large envelope through the post which Mrs Stuart had obviously mailed off to me after she had left my home that previous Saturday night. The necklace—the one I had seen in the crystal—was inside the envelope with a letter from Mrs Stuart saying that she wanted me to have it. Everything then began to fall into place—her pathetic fear . . . I still didn't know of whom she was afraid, but I now knew, or thought I knew, what this person had wanted from her. I'm sure you will understand how strongly I felt about the necklace . . . there had been so little that I could do for Mrs Stuart while she was alive, because of the terrible fear we now know she had of Mrs Keith . . . I couldn't close my eyes and pretend that it didn't matter to me: it did matter, very much . . . I simply had to do something about her murder; and the crystal had foretold that the necklace was the means to that end. Bullies, anyone who preys on another weaker than himself, are despicable, loathsome people. I shall always regret that I had so little time with Mrs Stuart, that she came to me so late in the day: but," she sighed, "it was not to be—"

Jean Sayer was nodding thoughtfully. "But you said that you saw danger in the crystal. Weren't you afraid?"

"I believe that each and every one of us is the master of our own individual destiny— Though," Mrs Charles said, almost in an aside, as she refilled Jean's cup, "it sometimes seems to me that few these days want the bother of charting their own course through life. I looked into the future and saw an indication of what lay ahead and from that knowledge came the strength to face up to that danger as and when it finally presented itself—if I chose, of course, to allow that danger to overtake me. The decision was mine: had I handed over the necklace to Mr Preston as he'd wanted, that would've been the end of it."

"How did he take your refusal to give it back?" Jean Sayer asked.

Mrs Charles smiled a little. "He didn't give up easily: but after a lot of talk, including the odd veiled threat or two of legal action, he finally went. I watched him leave from the window of my living-room. Walking up the street towards him was a woman: when they drew level with one another, they stopped and talked animatedly together. I thought the woman looked angry about something, or with him. Then they walked off. That woman was Cissie Keith. . . . Her hair was different in those days, longer and thicker and a beautiful, rich shade of red similar to the colour of Mrs Blackmore's hair . . . nothing like the appalling tint that Mrs Keith has put on her hair since going completely grey. She was also somewhat slimmer than she is today. I didn't see her face clearly—she and Mr Preston were some distance from the house when they stopped to talk—but there was a familiarity between them that was as immediately recognisable as any physical feature, even after the passage of all those years."

Jean Sayer looked at her husband. "Was Lionel Preston really Cissie's cousin?" she asked him.

"Yes," he replied. "It was through her that he got a job with the firm which employed her husband. Fred Church has been in touch with some other members of their family and Lionel Preston was apparently orphaned as a youngster and brought up by Cissie's mother. Cissie always had a strong hold over him. . . . He was forever in and out of scrapes on her account. The family also told Fred that they'd all thought that there was something odd about Cissie. There'd been some insanity on her father's side: a brother or a sister—nobody's sure which—finished up in a mental asylum, and the family suspected that Cissie would go that way, too."

"Was Lionel Preston involved with her in Janet Stuart's murder?" Jean asked.

"No," her husband replied. "It's almost certain he wasn't. Neither was her husband. He didn't wake up to what was going on until it was too late. He realised that she was mad and that the same thing would happen again—through his employment, he would be in a position to provide her with an endless stream of Mrs Stuarts—rich, defenceless, lonely old ladies—to prey on. There was nothing else for it: he had to retire, get Cissie as far away as possible from that kind of environment and its temptations."

"Why didn't he have her put away?" Jean wanted to know.

"I think," David said slowly, "for the simple reason that he loved her very dearly and felt that he could take care of her himself. But as we all know, he died not long after they settled here in the village, and with nobody to keep an eye on her the inevitable happened: she went after the money that everybody said Henrietta Player kept tucked away in her cottage."

Jean widened her eyes a little. "Your aunt has always insisted that Cissie was left fairly comfortably off."

"She was," he replied. "Her husband made more than adequate provision for her . . . that is, with the one exception: there was nothing he could do to safeguard her in the event of his death from her greatest need—"

"The *acquisition* of wealth," Mrs Charles said quietly for him. "It was a mania with her: she had no real need of Henrietta Player's money, but it was there, or was said to be there, and she had to have it."

Mrs Charles went on, for the moment addressing herself exclusively to Jean Sayer:

"On one particular occasion while Miss Player's son was at Whitethatch Cottage, he overheard snatches of a conversation which Miss Player was having with an-

other visitor . . . a woman, someone from the village was very nearly all that he seemed to know about
her—and that she appeared to be threatening his
mother in connection with a donation or donations to
the church. I naturally assumed that he was talking
about Mrs Blackmore who I knew to be in the habit
of making the occasional call on Mrs Player. I also
knew that through having met this man on one occasion at Whitethatch Cottage, Mrs Blackmore had been
able to give the police certain information concerning
him. However, he then went on to tell me about the
last occasion on which he saw his mother—which, as
you know, was the day she was murdered. The same
woman was there, and again he overheard her talking
to Miss Player in a very threatening, bullying tone of
voice. He went away without seeing or speaking to either one of them and returned some time later. That
was when he found his mother, Miss Player, dead. He
still had no idea who her other visitor, this woman,
was . . . except for being quite certain in his own
mind that she was someone from the village; but
when he went on to describe her hair to me—which
had made sufficient impression on him to cause him
to wonder, both at the time and afterwards, if she
wore a wig as some sort of disguise—there could be no
mistaking that he was referring to Mrs Keith. I could
think of no one else from the village with a hairstyle
which fitted the description he gave me—"

"Rusted wirewool?" Jean Sayer wryly wondered out
loud. "I could never understand why she didn't go to
a hairdresser and have her hair done properly: it
wasn't as though she couldn't afford it."

"Spending money, for any reason," her husband
said, "would be quite contrary to her nature. Anyone
with an obsession for money like hers is bound to be
mean with it."

Mrs Charles agreed and continued:

"I then realised my mistake about Mrs Blackmore and that first conversation which Miss Player's son overheard. It was Mrs Keith who was talking to Miss Player—I was completely wrong in thinking that it was Mrs Blackmore—and what he overheard was Mrs Keith accusing Miss Player of giving Mrs Blackmore money for the church while pretending to her, Mrs Keith, that she had no money at all. I suspect that Mrs Keith had hoped that by challenging her in this way, Miss Player would weaken and admit the existence of the money which she was rumoured to have. Soon after seeing Mrs Keith scooting off across the fields that day, Miss Player's son went back into the cottage and found someone else there with his mother: and that someone I have since come to realise was Mrs Blackmore, whose arrival had obviously hastened Mrs Keith's departure."

"What's going to happen about him . . . Miss Player's son?" Jean Sayer asked abruptly. "I mean, she didn't leave a will, did she? And if he really is her son, surely he'd have some right to her estate. No one else ever came forward to claim it."

"Steps were taken to administer the estate when no one put in a claim," David Sayer said, "which means that what money there is would now be held in Treasury Funds; and I think her son has every right to claim it within twelve years. He'd have to prove that Henrietta Player was his mother, but that shouldn't be too difficult: the home he was brought up in would have records of his birth."

"But what about the painting he stole?" Jean asked. "Won't he be charged with its theft?"

"I had a word with the Gidding boys about it yesterday afternoon," David replied. "I doubt if they'll be pressing any charges: not in the circumstances."

"I'm so glad," Mrs Charles said. "He made a big show of not caring anything for his mother, but deep down he did, despite her rejection of him."

"Whose murder do you think Cissie will be charged with?" Jean asked her husband. "Miss Player's? With the son's evidence it shouldn't be too difficult to get a conviction there."

"I rather think that Fred would like to have her charged with the Stuart murder, only because the necklace would be required as an exhibit at the trial and he wants a jeweller friend of his to have a look at it and tell him what it's worth," he grinned at Mrs Charles.

"But you don't feel it's very likely that she'll ever be charged with that murder—?" Jean guessed.

He shook his head. "I think the strongest case against her would probably be the murder of her cousin. The police have enough evidence there for a conviction . . . a top-coat they found hanging on a peg in the hall of her cottage had a few bloodstains on it which matched up with Preston's grouping, and the scrapings of mud and grass which were taken from a pair of her walking shoes put her right in the wood at the scene of the crime. . . . However, personally, I don't believe that she'll ever be brought to trail for any of the murders that she's committed. They're waiting on the psychiatric report now—" He shook his head again. "I can't see her ever coming out of hospital—there's never really been the slightest doubt about the sanity of the person who murdered Janet Stuart and Henrietta Player. . . ."

There was a long, reflective silence, and then suddenly David Sayer started to laugh. The two women looked at him expectantly.

"I was just thinking," he said after a moment. "This is the first time I've ever known Aunt Margaret to be lost for words: she simply didn't know what to say about poor Cissie."

"It must've been a very unpleasant shock for her," Mrs Charles commented. "I understand that they were quite close friends. . . . Perhaps," she went on thoughtfully, and her blue eyes twinkled a little, "I should drop round and see her sometime. I still have quite a bit of that strawberry jam left from last season. She might like a pot or two."

There was a pause and then they all laughed.

David Sayer cursed under his breath.

"What's wrong?" his wife asked, swinging her head round quickly to scan the narrow grey road which ribboned out behind them. "Have we run over something?"

"No—it's all right," he said abruptly. "I didn't mean to come this way."

"Why ever not? It's still the quickest way home, isn't it?"

They filtered on to the motorway.

"If you see him," David said grimly, staring fixedly ahead, "I don't want to know about it."

Jean laughed delightedly. "Of course . . . the Punch and Judy man. It's Wednesday!"

She ran her eye swiftly over the fields which bordered the motorway, but there was no sign anywhere of Cyril Forbes.

"You know . . ." her husband sighed at length, "if a hundred-yard section of this motorway ever goes missing, I for one will never need to wonder who got off with it!"

MIGNON WARNER, born in Adelaide, South Australia, now resides in England. She was a law clerk before turning to the pen. In addition to her writing, Ms. Warner assists her husband with his inventing, designing, and manufacturing of professional magic apparatus.

SCENE OF THE CRIME is the renowned mystery bookstore located in Sherman Oaks, California. Complete with turn-of-the-century decor, it specializes in literature of crime, detection, intrigue, and mystery. A Medium for Murder has been selected by Ms. Ruth Winfeldt, proprietor of Scene of the Crime, and editorial consultant for the Dell Scene of the Crime™ mystery series.